FIFTY THOUSAND YEARS . . .

Time is a river that twists on itself. Past, present and future are its waters—mixing, separating, and remixing. And the fluid of time is life. When life ceases to exist time becomes meaningless. We are the protectors of life. Now you will see and understand.

Jason came to in the car. He was still looking into the other man's eyes . . . eyes that had veiled themselves again in fathomless green.

"Do you understand now, Mr. Starr?"

"I think so. If there was only one man who survived the—sleep—and he was the one who created the time-traveling device . . . then you must be that man!"

"Approximately correct. Certain changes were necessary. Only the brain was preserved. My brain was transplanted." The stranger's voice was low and far away.

Fifty thousand years away, Jason thought in awe.

THE MIND BROTHERS

PETER HEATH

PRESTIGE BOOKS • NEW YORK

THE MIND BROTHERS

PRESTIGE BOOKS INC. • 18 EAST 41ST STREET
NEW YORK, N.Y. 10017

Chapter 1
ONE

A BLOOD-RED SUN swam up through the marsh fog until the heat churned it into a vivid crimson soup. The huge disk floated higher and, clearing the last tendrils of mist, it hung on the edge of the world; then it began to climb its arc. Already, its monsoon-making heat was felt in the never-sleeping city. A city where the French had once ruled an empire of rubber, coffee and corruption in their voluble, charming and decadent way. A city where now the Americans sat in sweat-stained fatigues toasting the sunrise with stale warm beer and tried hard not to think about anything.

No one slept in Saigon . . . unless it was after they had had a girl, or were just plain exhausted. There was too much to do and too much to forget. The great city at the mouth of the sluggish river had once been called the Paris of the East. Now it was an inlet and an outlet for men and the machinery of destruction; a great heart, pumping supplies uphill to the dirty war that raged so closely around it; so closely that at night you could hear the mortar fire in the liquid darkness. So close that planes landing at Saigon International Airport could fly a mission without a scratch and yet land with neat rows of holes stitched across their wings—put there by the Vietcong seamstresses holed up under the approach pattern.

But the heart continued to pump. In spite of the confusion, bad planning, dirt, heat, danger and death, the twin sun-bleached runways served their current masters faithfully and the morning air was full of the whine of turbines, the cough of cold pistons and the stench of burnt rubber, exhaust and raw gasoline.

The sun was up now, and no one except the Vietnamese in the control tower even bothered to look at the tiny, single-engined Air Force L-19 as it taxied out of its revetment. It was just another battle-chewed old kite . . . going somewhere and who the hell cared? Probably not even the two dirty and tired men inside.

The L-19 chugged slowly down a long line of heavily guarded F-105 Thunderchiefs, aswarm with maintainance crews and ordinance teams. Then it bumped past a squadron of Gooney Birds loading a company of South Vietnamese Rangers, little men with huge American packs on their wiry backs. They were being hustled aboard by a Special Forces Sergeant with a silver whistle on a cord around his neck, while the helicopter blades whirled silver against the sun.

At last the L-19 joined the end of the long waiting line, behind a flight of four F-104 Starfighters. It waited there, its engine already overheated, and the colonel in the observer's seat and the captain at the controls tried to stay awake under the sweltering plexiglass.

The fact that the L-19 wasn't just another puddlejumper on a Rec and Search mission and the fact that the cargo it carried was worth thousands of man-hours and more than its weight in diamonds might have disturbed the grease monkeys and the technicians who had spent the night tearing the guts out of the number two engine of the C-141 Starlifter parked near the end of the runway. But it was doubtful. They were sound asleep in the shadow cast by one of its immense wings.

But if they had known what the strong-jawed, gray-eyed young man with the sensitive lips who was riding in the back seat knew, they might have had nightmares instead of fantasies about the women Saigon or their wives, girlfriends and mistresses back in the States.

The flight of F-104's moved up to the apron. Nasty silver birds with wings like sawed-off shotguns. Short range, immense speed and with the firepower of a battleship. They were the hunters.

"The Eagle Scouts are waitin' fer their li'l ol' exercise," the precise southern voice of the commander of the F-104's drawled through the command channel, jolting both of the half-dozing men in the L-19 back into reality.

"Roger and count-down your roll from ten seconds . . . Mark," a voice with an Oriental tinge replied. With its overloaded facilities, Saigon Airport had to time its landings and takeoffs to the split second.

"We're rollin'," the young southerner sang out. Simultaneously, four J-79 jet engines wound up to maximum rpm's and four after-burners kicked in with great blasts of yellow flame. The 104's crouched and sprang forward. First slowly, then faster. Suddenly they were a silver blur far down the runway.

"Our turn coming up, Colonel." The captain half turned in his seat, and Jason Starr nodded his head.

"Gears up and climbing," the lieutenant's voice came in clearly. It was thirty-five seconds and ten miles away and the F-104's were shooting straight up at approximately 1,350 miles per hour.

Now it was the L-19's turn. The captain gave her the gun. Unbalanced and slightly overloaded with the instrumentation that Starr had sweated and cursed all night long to install, she slithered and mushed along, gaining speed so slowly that Starr's fists clenched into tight balls and his toes curled up inside the old tennis shoes that he had worn in place of the uncomfortable Air Force version of the jungle boot.

But the captain knew his business—which was exactly why the AFSWR had yanked him out of the cockpit of an X-15 rocket plane for this mission. After what seemed an interminable period of engine roar and runway jounce, she floated off, her flaps slid into their dirty grease-covered slots, her nose came down, and she banked hard to the left, away from the concrete and away from an incoming Pan American Airlines 707, which had already touched down and was braking to a stop beneath them.

They throttled back, and Jason Starr, his lanky but muscular body crimped into a knot in the tight cockpit, allowed himself a somewhat boyish grin. Project Hysteria was off the ground and on its way toward a patch of jungle a hundred and twenty miles away—a patch of jungle that might change the history of the world. For the contents of the three black boxes that he had welded to the steel tubing of the airframe, where his sensitive fingers could play over their dial- and switch-studded faces, were certainly going to change something. It had been worth it, Starr decided —the lack of sleep, the heat, even the absence of women.

Now, as the L-19 puttered along, its flimsy wings jiggling through the low altitude turbulence, he let his thoughts ride elsewhere.

He slipped back through the months of high-speed computational engineering in the Air Force Special Weapons Research Center, a bleak place in the high

Rockies where no one was invited unless his services were first classified as vital . . . all the way back to the quiet days in his office at the RAND Corporation in Santa Monica, California. To his house in Pacific Palisades, with its view of the ocean, its library and its garage full of high-performance sports cars. And the nights on the patio, with women in his arms, making love, broiling steaks and playing the big-little games of love until the sun came up through the morning's haze.

He missed it, but he had left it by choice and without a backward glance. When the man from the Air Force Special Weapons Research Center had walked into his office, lit his pipe and told him to pack his bags, "Colonel Starr" had been born. The rank was a politeness extended by the Department of Defense to the men it requisitioned for its mental stockpile.

Naturally, Jason's first reaction had been hostile.

"Look, whoever you are, I don't go anywhere for anybody unless they have a pretty good reason . . . a damn good reason," he said bluntly. "Spent too much time learning how to think for myself to waste it," he added.

"It won't be wasted, Doctor Starr," the AFSWR man said. "The Special Weapons Research Center isn't in the habit of wasting people's time."

"That's what you say." Jason rose from his desk and crossed the office to the steel-slatted security window. Through the slits he could see the summer sun whitewashing the street below. "I'm thirty-two years old, I'm engaged in highly classified research for a semi-independent agency of the U.S. Government, I have two Ph.D.'s and a master's degree . . . and I like it. I like the money, I like the work, and I like being a civilian."

9

"Yes, we know all that, Doctor, and that's why I'm here. We know how you feel about war and, more specifically, what you're doing to think of alternative solutions," said the AFSWR man.

"Well—?"

"Just that your services on this particular *project* could make the difference between—shall we say— survival or extinction of the human race."

Jason's eyebrows raised. "Cleaner H-bombs?" he said. "—sorry."

"Hardly, Doctor. I mean saving lives."

"Project what?" Jason was half-hooked by then and he knew it.

"Project Hysteria." The AFSWR man's face was shadowed, gloomy, cold. He looked as if he hadn't slept in a month or two.

"Until you say yes or no, I can't be too specific, Doctor. For several years the Department of Defense has been developing a device which has involved the best scientific minds in the country. Progress has been made. Now we need a computer specialist to clear the last hurdle . . . a computer specialist of the highest order. That's you, Doctor Starr."

"What if I say yes?" said Jason softly.

"You'll work completely alone. The others never knew the full implications of what they were doing, but you will—and you'll be responsible for testing the equipment."

"And just what is Project Hysteria?" asked Jason.

The room was absolutely quiet. The air conditioning hummed tunelessly. Jason's eyes were fixed on the AFSWR man's tired-out face.

"Thought control, Doctor," he replied.

A thermal updraft hit the L-19 in the belly. It shied sideways like a frightened colt and the engine screamed in protest. Jason looked down. Now they were skimming over a solid green carpet, the jungle boudoir of the Vietcong. Even at 130 miles per hour the smell of rotting vegetation and stagnant water filtered into the sweltering cockpit. The captain cursed sourly while he tried to keep the plane level and read his maps at the same time.

· "We'll be over the target grid in zero eight minutes," he announced.

Jason gave him thumbs-up. It was easier than trying to shout over the wind and engine noise. He checked out the systems, flicking switches, adjusting voltages, checking and rechecking circuits until there was only one more switch to throw—a black toggle protected by a red safety guard. The words: TRIGGER, DANGEROUS WHEN ACTIVATED were stenciled neatly underneath.

Jason grinned at that. No one knew whether it was dangerous or not. The closest the Air Force had gotten to it was to stick on the label. It was a collection of instruments designed by a high-speed computer which analyzed the information that Jason laboriously fed into it and came up with an answer. An answer that not even he, with fifteen years of theoretical mathematics, could completely understand.

The coming test would prove whether or not a combination of transistors, wires and dish antennas could broadcast the emotions of fear, confusion and frustration to a selected group of human minds. It was a test being carried out in such complete secrecy that not even the CIA or Air Force Intelligence had been informed.

If the thing worked he would know soon enough. Just as he had made rats, birds and monkeys go berserk under controlled laboratory conditions, he expected to make people—normal human beings—respond in the same way. Seen in physical terms, the brain is nothing more nor less than a computer made out of living tissue—brain cells. And, like man-made computers, the brain uses electrical energy to function. The equipment that Jason had designed duplicated and amplified brain waves and broadcast them on the same frequencies that living brains used during the thinking process. Theoretically, the equipment could broadcast any pattern of waves in any combination. However, Jason had worked against the deadline imposed by the Air Force and he had confined his experiments to the instantaneous conditioning of animals. In its current state of development the machine was limited to one major "program." It transmitted fear. The kind of primitive fear that was beyond the level of the conscious mind. The kind of fear that would make men forget their pride, their duty and their identities. The kind of fear that would make them utterly useless as soldiers. If it worked, war, as a way of solving humanity's quarrels, was finished for good.

He had arrived in Saigon alone with a couple of crates and some orders assigning him the L-19 and its pilot. The captain up front was in the dark as far as the nature of the equipment was concerned. His job was to get the puddle-jumper over the target. And Jason's job was to push the buttons in the right ways and get himself back to Saigon . . . to wait for the results. The results would be investigated by the Special Forces team he had requisitioned from the Special Warfare Center in Saigon. They were now hovering ten miles away in a fleet of whirlybirds, waiting to move in at his radio command.

In the laboratory the effects had been temporary. Jason hoped the same was true in the field. At best it was a grim business, and he was happy to be on the shielded side of the directional antennas installed under the tail of the L-19.

"Pow! . . . as they say on *Batman*," the captain shouted over his shoulder. "We're coming up on target, sir."

The green velvet jungle looked the same. But a mile ahead Starr caught a swift glimpse of a river running silver through the tropical forest. There was a patch of brown bordering it—the clearing and huts of a small Vietcong unit—the perfect target for Project Hysteria's test.

The L-19 banked ninety degrees to the left, lining up on the treetops that fringed the edge of the river. Jason bounced his head against the canopy as the little craft leveled off and then went into a short, steep climb to lose airspeed. The nose swung down again, the engine backfired once as it was throttled back, and they were mushing in over the river . . . so low that Jason could see a school of minnows scampering away from their moving shadow.

His hand found the trigger guard and flipped it up. The clearing was around a sharp bend a half-mile ahead. The plane purred toward its rendezvous, threading the needle-path between the high jungle trees that closed off escape from both sides. Jason knew, then, what a bombardier felt in his guts: a savage state of calm excitement. His finger crooked around the toggle. The L-19 swept into its turn, one wingtip brushing a few inches above the water. Now he could see the clearing just ahead—calm and empty under the afternoon sun. His finger began to pull the switch. It never finished the task.

They had waited for three hours. The two U.S. Army .50-caliber machine guns—captured months ago from an ambushed truck convoy—were set up on opposite banks of the river, their fields of fire crossing in the center. They had posted observers with walkie-talkies far up the river. They had known well in advance what to look for and when to be ready.

The men looked like regular North Vietnamese; the village gave the impression it was intended to give; and Colonel Po had organized and executed his mission along classic guerilla lines. His men had been infiltrated with regular units and he had walked the Ho Chi Minh trail with three other colonels, bound for new assignments with tactical regiments. It had taken them two months to assemble, to build the small village, and to wait.

And now the purpose of their operation approached.

As the L-19 skidded out of its turn, Po's arm came up. He grinned wolfishly.

"Aim carefully, comrades," he shouted in Chinese. His arm snapped down.

Two streams of tracers converged into a single point fifty feet ahead of the plane. At seventy miles an hour, even an L-19 is barely flying. But it is moving too fast for a human to react instantaneously. The captain saw the white puffs and identified them. In a movement too swift to follow, he hit the throttle and pulled back on the stick. Only three-quarters of a second had elapsed, but the captain was too late.

The L-19 flew through a hail of lead and things happened even more swiftly. The plane was rising when the first bullets tore through its flimsy fuselage. Instead of ripping the engine to shreds and shattering the windscreen, they splattered into the belly with a series of vibrating explosions under the floorboards that sounded like hail. The L-19's control cables were sheared, locking the horizontal and vertical stabilizers

14

into the position the captain had instinctively chosen —a steep climb.

It happened so quickly that Jason was still reacting to the captain's first curse when the L-19 entered the swarm of bullets. Then something smashed him in the thigh with the power of a mule's kick and his mind grew hazy. The engine was roaring wide open and they seemed to be climbing steeply. He was aware of something sticky and warm on the numbness of his right leg . His hand was still on the toggle. He looked at it. It all seemed part of a dream, and he continued to watch it unfold with strange amusement.

With its engine wide open, the L-19 nosed up into the sky. It rose quickly away from the river and the running men on the ground. Swiftly, the men receded until they were no longer men but tiny toys, waving their arms ridiculously and looking upward. Jason laughed. It seemed very funny. He wondered if the captain up front appreciated the humor. He decided to ask him.

But the captain seemed very busy. He was hunched over the controls keeping the nose pointed toward the great silver sun that had appeared in front of Jason's eyes. I must ask him, he thought. He leaned forward and tapped the captain's shoulder. Then he tugged. Then he pulled. Finally the captain leaned back and Jason could see the gaping, Y-shaped hole where the captain's forehead had been.

Jason wanted to say something. A word of comfort to make the captain feel better. But he couldn't stop laughing.

Then an overworked oil line burst and the engine stopped. The captain, who was quite dead, fell forward as the plane now began its plunge toward the green jungle 1,500 feet below. Jason watched the jungle rise swiftly. He heard the shrill whine of the wind through the aluminum struts. Then the L-19 began to spin, and the whole world became a green vortex. The whine rose to a hysterical level. Then Jason remembered . . . the switch . . . he was supposed to do something with it. Five seconds before the L-19 dug its grave in the jungle floor his fingers were still fumbling.

Then there was no more world and no more anything.

Chapter †
TWO

A THIN STREAK of blue marked the top of the rain forest. A green fly hovered in the cool shadow. It was investigating the twisted mass of wreckage that lay in the deep gash carved in the red earth. It came closer. It buzzed a hunger sound. Then it settled on the protruding arm closest to the shade and it began to feed.

Since the creature was too small to interfere with the transfer facility, it was left alone. The air shimmered five feet away from the crater. It pulsed rapidly and an almost invisible blue light played across a growing spot. The spot became a definable circle, poised five feet above the surface of the jungle floor. It changed to a deeper blue and grew outward. Slowly, it dilated until it was a lens six feet in diameter. The lens was limitlessly deep, a vortex of pure force, shimmering and vibrating in the cool shadows.

The fly continued to suck the coagulated blood out of the open wound on the arm. Since its eyes operated on the infrared spectrum and its ears in the ultrasonic range, it sensed nothing as the lens began to move. The lens moved slowly and delicately until it hovered over the wreckage of the airplane. It paused for a few seconds. Then it descended until it enclosed what remained of the rear section and what remained of the man inside.

The fly was quite content. Suddenly it emitted a shrill buzz of anger and frustration. The arm and the body it was attached to were gone. The loud pop of air rushing in to fill a small vacuum drove the fly five feet away. All was quiet. It waited and then it flew toward the other bloody but edible thing and settled to its interrupted meal.

By the time the first crackle of foliage announced the coming of humans, the fly had bloated itself and had flown away. Colonel Po and his men came out of the jungle with trained caution. Without a word, his specialists went to work. By the time they had finished their task, the first sound of American helicopter motors could be heard in the distance. With a quick glance at the sky, Po ordered his men back into the jungle. Then, with an American safety match, Po ignited one of the L-19's ruptured wing tanks. He waited until the smoke billowed high enough to mark the wreckage. Then he too faded into the forest.

The body lay inside a transparent cube while probes analyzed the extent of its damage and prepared the repair apparatus. A steady hum filled the vast interior of the Transfer Facility. Robotlike tentacles moved in the shadows. A thousand lights winked their different-colored messages across the faces of the instruments. Outside the air was warm and scented, the perpetual spring on the night face of the planet.

The analyzer finished its investigation. Now it issued its instructions. New energies were created and focused to points deep within the still body. Atoms altered their positions slightly; new molecules were formed; chromosomes and gene chains re-spiraled themselves until the analyzer was satisfied. A part of the dead brain was energized and instructed to repair the internal and external damage. It did this aided

18

by the instruments a million times more swiftly than it could have done under normal circumstances. The energy and direction was supplied by the machine.

Even so, the repairs were extensive. It took the machine five minutes to complete them. And still the body lay cold inside the evacuated cube with the supervisors watching, checking and waiting.

Now the machine issued its final instructions. Gases—oxygen, nitrogen and minute quantities of argon and helium—were created. They boiled out of micro-pores into the cube until the atmosphere of Earth in the twentieth century was expanding and steaming over the inert body. Then the machine issued a command that the bio-physicists of the year 51,220 A.D. had studied intensively as children . . . a command that galvanized the processes into a whole. A command that produced a succession of twitches in the long-dormant heart muscle, twitches which organized themselves into the first full systolic contraction.

Jason Starr opened his eyes.

He wanted to scream. He was floating almost weightlessly inside of a glass box, something that reminded him of an aquarium, and he was utterly naked. His senses seemed totally disoriented. He was afraid. He wanted to be a child again. Because, on the other side of the aquarium wall, there was blackness; and in the blackness he saw *something* staring at him.

The analyzer reported the fear the second it was generated. A command was given immediately.

Suddenly the walls which enclosed Jason changed to opaque. His weight returned and he was lying on his back, breathing fresh pure air. A soft light filled the chamber, its source a mystery.

Jason tried to sit up, but not a muscle would obey. It was an inward block, as if the part of his mind that issued instructions to his body was being over-ridden by a force too powerful to resist. The same force seemed to be controlling his respiration. As he watched the regular rise and fall of his chest, memory returned.

The plane, plunging toward the green jungle. The pilot dead. His finger trying to throw the switch . . . then nothing. And now—? It was totally beyond anything he had ever experienced. It was as if . . .

But Jason never finished the thought. A voice was growing. A voice inside of him. A voice that wasn't like anything he had ever heard before.

You are called Jason Starr, it said. *Do not be afraid. I have—transported—you in order to repair your damaged systems. Do you understand?*

Repair his damaged systems? Sweat broke out on Jason's forehead. A twisted, broken bundle of dead flesh inside the shattered L-19 . . . and now he was in one piece . . . he was breathing . . . his body felt normal, even relaxed. Something had prevented him from dying . . . or at least from staying dead.

"What—are—you?" He mouthed the words, knowing that the *thing* had different ears—mental ears.

It will be explained at the proper time, the voice filled his mind. *I have recreated you in order to serve your race. Your existence is necessary on the M-27 time plane. You will be returned shortly. Your world line will continue.*

The enormity of the statement sank into Jason's mind. For centuries man had speculated on the possibilities of time travel; for the past fifty years the world's greatest scientific minds had given the question serious study. But no one had proven or dis-proven Einstein's postulates on the subject. And now Jason was communicating with an intelligent being

20

who seemed to be able to penetrate the envelope of past, present and future.

"Can you explain who—what—you are?" he said, this time as coolly as possible.

It will be explained at the proper time. First you must agree to return to your continuum as my ally. The voice, or whatever it was, seemed to be waiting for a reply.

Jason had the feeling that his decision could make the difference between life and death. Death number two, he thought. Or hallucination number three, a crazy mixed-up dream with voices in his head, something peering through transparent walls at him . . . a million laughs . . . what a way to go. Except that he knew it wasn't a dream. It was happening.

If he said no—would he ever wake up? If he said yes, would his world be the old familiar one with his work, his pleasures and a life expectancy of seventy-five? In the last analysis there could be only one answer. Forever is a long, long time.

"Yes," he said. "I agree to help you, or is it serve you?"

You were chosen because of your intelligence. You were chosen not to obey but to act according to your decisions.

"So now what happens?"

You will return to your continuum. You will resume your human functions. You will forget . . . until contact is made again.

"Forget! But why?" A thought crossed Jason's mind. Before he could ask his next question the *thing* interrupted.

You will be contacted at the appropriate time. Until then, resume your normal pattern.

He was being lifted by mandibles of force that

were so strong yet so gentle that he felt like a baby starting its passage from the womb into the world. Then he was spinning, faster and faster, into a tunnel of blackness. When the blackness was so thick that it seemed to penetrate his body, he lost consciousness. His last thought was: forever is a long, long, long time.

The Special Forces reconnaissance team found the still-smoldering wreckage of the L-19 in the dark. They found it by using their noses.

It wasn't a pretty smell. The stench of burnt flesh never is. The thing that had been the pilot was an unrecognizable lump of charcoal, smashed into the remaining pieces of the instrument panel.

"It isn't much of a thought but thank God the poor bastard was dead before the fire started," said the tall officer with no bars on his lapel.

"Captain, I've seen some smash-ups in my time but never one like this," said a sergeant with no stripes. "Probably hit nose-down with the controls locked. Looks like they really opened up on her. They never had a chance."

The captain grunted. It was strange. Not the way the L-19 had crashed—they got it the same way every day—and not the poor bastard in the front seat. What was screwy was the man they had found sprawled nearby, his parachute unopened, his body apparently undamaged and his breathing deep and regular. In a deep coma, a colonel in the Air Force . . . now what in the hell was he doing alive when he should have been pulverized in the crash? The captain adjusted his holstered .45. He looked up at the star-strewn night sky, a habit he had fallen into during his five years of jungle combat. Five years dur-

22

ing which he had seen more than a man cares to re-member.

At last he shrugged. "Well, let's stop scratching our armpits," he growled at his men. "The joker was lucky but he's not lucky enough to keep living unless we shovel him up and get him back to the medics. And salvage what you can of that junk in the rear seat. We were supposed to provide verification of damages and I guess the Air Force will want some evidence." The captain flicked off the tip of his cigarette and his men went to work.

Chapter †
THREE

THE SUN was shining through a window and the air was so sweet that he could taste it. Light. Taste? A jumble of other sensations entered Jason Starr's mind as it groped its way up from blackness. The pillow, the soft sheets, the faint smell of medicinals. A hospital. Of course. He opened his eyes.

He was lying in a high-ceilinged room, facing two big windows that opened onto a scene that he knew well: blue sky, green hills above, and ships—hundreds of them—moving and anchored in the land-locked harbor below. In between, rows of neat bungalows on wide, tree-shaded streets. He was in the Navy Hospital at Pearl Harbor. He tried to sit up. It was a dizzying process, and he let himself sink slowly back. Memory was shot to hell: an aching confusion of half-real, half-crazy dreams and the strange stirrings of something so deeply buried in his subconscious that it was like the recollection of another life. It was like trying to remember being born.

He sighed and slept again—this time the normal sleep of a man who had returned from the eternal, sad sleep of death. As twilight crept over the green hills the nurse tiptoed into the room. She closed the Venetian blinds and stood looking down at the sun-etched face of the sleeper. It was a strong and yet tender face. The well-molded lips had the slight curl upward that indicated both humor and natural sensuality. It was an experienced and strong face, she thought. No woman would ever know it completely. She was a woman who knew men. She leaned over him and her lips brushed his. Then she left.

The CIA men came early the next morning. Two of them, both young and both with that look of professional distrust that always put them apart from other, more normal young men. They took Starr into an empty doctor's office. Then they talked to him.

"The Air Force has decided to write Project Hysteria off, Colonel," said the crewcut blond one. "So you're going back to your old job . . . if you still want it, of course. No one will ask any questions, so you don't have to worry on that score."

Just like that. You were told to forget it and you forgot.

"Now wait one hundred million minutes," said Starr. "You're telling me the project is headed for the wastebasket! Without even a test! Millions of dollars, thousands of man-hours, and you don't even want to know if the thing really works?"

He scowled blackly across the desk. The blond one wasn't having any. Jason continued, "I want a better explanation. I want some facts . . . so forget that you're little-boy spies long enough to tell me what I'm doing in a Navy Hospital. And how the hell the Air Force decided to cancel out five months of hard work."

The ball was passed to the other one, with the pipe in his breast pocket. Very collegiate, no doubt. A real Yale paratrooper.

"That's what we're afraid of, Colonel. Or do you prefer me to call you Doctor . . . ?" He waited.

When nothing happened he went on: "Look—ah—Doctor . . . the Air Force did recruit you to produce some kind of machine—even we don't know what. According to our information you worked alone. And now the Air Force says it's canceling the whole business. We were sent here to tell you. Your work is finished. Here—" The unsmiling youngster drew a large white envelope out of his inside pocket. "Inside, you'll find discharge papers—honorable, of course—a plane ticket to the West Coast . . . and—a—" The CIA man cleared his throat. He was embarrassed. "A *compensatory* sum of money for services rendered above and beyond the call of duty. It's made out to your bank in Los Angeles."

So they used me, thought Jason, body and brain for five months. And now the big payoff. Now you can go home and forget you ever knew us. Because we're the big boys, we make the rules and we control the action. And we're shipping you back to the minor leagues.

"Sorry," he said quietly and calmly. "I have other plans in mind. You want to hear them? Oh, I forgot. You don't know anything so you wouldn't be able to give me any advice. So I'll skip the juicy parts and you'll understand. In fact, now that I think about it, you'll both be able to read about them in the newspapers." Starr allowed himself to smile. The message was getting across. The two junior-executive espionage agents were looking uncomfortably at each other.

There was a bit of throat clearing, finger twitching, pocket adjusting, and silence. The type with the pipe finally let his jaw relax enough to sigh.

Then he said, "I was hoping that it wouldn't be necessary, Doctor Starr. But since you seem unwilling to take our advice in this matter, you should at least be aware of the consequences of such—rashness." The word fell out of his face like a rock.

"What are you saying?" For the first time, Starr felt a sinking feeling.

"The contents of the cases, Doctor . . ." The CIA man let the sentence dangle in mid air.

"Highly sophisticated electronic components. Show me a Class Q Clearance, tell me you have a 'need to know,' and I'll tell you how they functioned."

"That won't be necessary, Doctor. We already know."

"What?"

"Sorry to have to be the one, Doctor. But you know as well as I—*the boxes had no function.*"

"You're crazy." Starr looked into the blue eyes across the desk. They were calm, assured, even friendly.

"Doctor, when the Special Forces team picked you up out of the jungle, they salvaged the instruments you had installed. They were flown back to Washington for analysis in our labs at Air Force request. Do you want to know what our best electron specialists had to say, Doctor? I'll tell you. The wires, tubes, transistors and batteries of your so-called 'device' added up to a great big fat nothing. In fact, all they did was produce dial indications and glowing green and red lights . . . So if you want to present your case to the papers, that's up to you. It's your reputation, not ours. If you've changed your mind, then we're willing to let the whole matter drop."

"Since you seem to know what the equipment was designed to do, what about the tests in Colorado?" Jason played his last card. "They showed what the machine could do," he said.

"They showed the symptoms of something, Doctor. According to our report, the *something* was probably LSD, a drug that produces that kind of hallucinations that your—a—machine was supposed to create. You worked by yourself, Doctor. It would have been easy for someone—we don't necessarily mean you—to give the animals an injection." The CIA man paused. He looked at his watch. He stood up. His friend followed suit.

"Now, Doctor, I think you understand your position. If—" his hand indicated the envelope. "—if you decide to accept the contents we will all be very grateful. And I see we have a flight to catch. Goodbye, Doctor . . . and good luck."

Jason said nothing as the two men left. He sat staring at the envelope. Then he stared at the wall. At last he stood up. He put the envelope into his bathrobe pocket and went back to his room. There he lay on his bed and stared some more.

The squeeze was on from all directions. Someone was pulling off one of the most fantastic frame-ups in history. Perhaps it was his own government, perhaps not. But it was a mystery that would haunt him for the rest of his life. And what kind of a life could he lead with the knowledge that his government would never trust him again? Not on the big things, not as a scientist or even as a man. There had to be a logical explanation. But how to find it or even where to begin looking was the question.

He closed his eyes and let his mind roam back. The plane spinning out of control and now the hospital. That was all. But *something*. In some way there was more. He concentrated until his thoughts flew off in all directions again. It was a blank wall. He could feel it in him like an itch, and it wouldn't go away.

"Welcome back to the living," a throaty feminine voice said.

He turned his head slowly in the direction of the

door. She had splendid legs, brown eyes, and a sense of humor. He decided he'd like to get to know her better, and in order to do so tried to sit up.

It was a dizzying process. By the time he'd made it, her soft arms were around him, the delicious smell of her hair was saturating his senses, and he let himself be lifted gently toward the edge of the bed. Together they managed the long climb from the horizontal to the vertical, and, when he was finished sitting up, he found her ivory neck so invitingly close that he had to kiss it.

"Hey. You aren't supposed to feel good enough to do things like that," the nurse breathed against his ear. She extracted herself slowly.

"I'm welcoming myself home," said Jason with a smile which told her enough to make a slow blush spread across her high-cheekboned face. Together they laughed, and the nurse let her imagination roam over the strong, tanned body of the man whom she had known so intimately but chastely over the past few days. The thought excited her, so she changed the subject.

"Do you know where you are?" she asked.

" 'Fraid so. Spent some time here testing weapons systems for the Navy five years ago. The Navy Hospital. Pearl Harbor. But what in Hell's name am I doing here?" Jason let the suspicions that had been forming dominate his thoughts for the moment.

"Well, you've been in a very sound sleep—or what we call a deep coma—for the past two weeks."

He let the information sink in. "All right," he said, "great. Then maybe you can tell me why a colonel in the U.S. Air Force is being kept in a Navy facility instead of an Air Force boneyard!"

"That, sir, you'll have to ask someone else." She winked at him as if it were a children's game and they

29

were both in on the secret. Starr gave up for the moment. She was a very pretty girl. He decided to say something silly.

"Tell you what—when I find out, you and I can whisper it to each other in the dark," he said.

"Hmmm—that might be very interesting," she chuckled. "But it doesn't have to be in the dark. I've been changing your sheets, pajamas and bedpans for the last fourteen days!"

She squeezed his arm playfully.

"Well, you should've changed my character while you were at it—apparently the government doesn't trust it any more," he said.

"People can make mistakes." The nurse turned at the door and their eyes met briefly.

"I'll vote for that," said Jason, sinking back and closing his eyes.

Chapter †
FOUR

THE TWO TENNIS PLAYERS looked across the net at each other. One was smiling, the other glaring, while the audience—one former movie queen, slightly old, with super-size sunglasses, one lacquer-blonde mistress of several film producers and one teenaged Lolita—tried hard not to laugh.

The day was hot and smog-ridden. The sinewy club pro, the man whose twenty-five thousand dollars a year depended on his ability to beat and teach out-of-shape amateurs, was angry. He was being beaten and beaten badly.

The man across from him, the one with the wheat-colored hair and the muscle-dancing tanned body, had taken the pro's game apart piece by piece. Now he was brilliantly slamming them all back with sheer animal enjoyment. The pro knew he was good and hated him for it. The pro had once been the national men's singles champion, and to lose to an amateur was hard. To lose in front of women was even harder.

Now, with a grunt of anger, the pro served. The next point was match point, and he gave the ball everything he had. He raced to cut off the expected weak return at the net. It was the standard tactic; it worked with good amateurs and better professionals. But it only worked when the return was easy to handle. The pro was only in his second stride when the ball whizzed by his ear with a faint humming sound. It dropped precisely on top of the back-court line. The game was over.

The pro threw his racket down in disgust and turned to look at the winner.

"Where did you learn your tennis, buddy?" he demanded.

"Not at the Beverly Hills Tennis Club," said Jason. "Couldn't afford it when I was a kid."

"Neither could I," the pro agreed. He picked up his racket and walked toward Jason with his hand out.

"Sorry I got carried away. You know how it is—people with so much dough dripping out of their pockets that you have to make them look good or you might as well forget about your job," he said.

They shook hands, and Jason set about retrieving his balls.

He was pulling on his sweater when a voice that was a study in provocation said: "That was wild, whatever your name is. I'll bet you do lots of other wild things, too."

Jason pulled the sweater down and opened his eyes. Yes, it was the Lolita, pouting up at him, lips half-open, legs quivering as if they were on a postage-stamp dance floor, eyes traveling up and down his body like searchlights looking for an escaped convict. She was the go-go girl of 1967, and Jason wasn't interested.

"Never mind what I do, baby-doll," he said. "When you grow up to be eighteen and a half and learn how to chew your food properly—then maybe we'll have a discussion."

She pouted her disappointment at him. He ran the gauntlet of sex-hungry glances without a word, through the gate opening on to the drive where his

32

car was parked. He tossed his racket and balls under the tonneau of the Porsche, got in, started the engine . . . and sat.

It was cooling down, and a little fog was creeping in from the beach towns. It was drink time, woman time, play time. It was time to lie outside on his patio, looking down at the Pacific and listening to Beethoven and rehashing the day's work at the RAND Corporation. These were the things he had done in the past with the fullest pleasure. And now he wasn't interested any more.

Women? What woman wants a man whose reputation has been questioned? Oh, of course, there were the easy girls, but no one who mattered. The one who had mattered—she had promised him she would wait no matter how long he was gone—had suddenly quit her job with RAND. She had left a note for him. It said: "I'm sorry, Jason, it's no good anymore. Forgive me . . ."

And then the job. No problems. He had resigned it a week ago. It was the only choice, and he had taken it.

Scientists and mathematicians are as inbred as a baseball team. They travel a lot, and a word here and a word there from the *right* sources is all that it takes to put together the facts. Somehow the word was out. Perhaps the CIA had decided to let it out themselves. It was the story of a man suspected of a breach of ethics on a secret project. Nothing specific . . . . nothing proved . . . but there it was. He, Jason Starr, couldn't be trusted. And in his line of work, trust was a most important factor.

He was frozen out, and he knew it. They had killed the old life and, with it, the old Jason—the enthusiast for every idea, every project. In his place they had created a brooding man who sat for long hours in his

33

darkened office with the door closed. A man suddenly without friends and without work.

With a savage jerk he threw the car into first and screamed away from the curb, leaving a trail of smoking rubber. He drove home, going up Sunset Boulevard, passing the evening traffic on curves and straights with equal recklessness until he was alone. He left the car in the driveway and showered and changed clothes hastily. Then he drove more slowly back down toward Beverly Hills and the Sunset Strip.

He sat, nursing a Scotch, with his back against the leather-tooled wallpaper in the dimmest corner of the Via Veneto watching the young swingers in their nightly performance. The hip little girls with the extra-long hair, sylph-like bodies and pretty, oyster-sized mouths. And their boyfriends with Beatle haircuts, pipestem pants and cool ideas. The action was just getting under way, and he let his eyes flicker over to the golden-haired Circe whose eyes had been playing tricks with him across the circular fireplace for the past half-hour. She smiled invitingly and Jason winked no thanks.

Ordinarily he would have gone to her and made a few pleasantly suggestive remarks, and they would have driven up to the house in his black Porsche to spend the night in play and chatter.

But tonight, as on most of the nights since he had been back into the civilian world, his mind was somewhere else. In his inner world—a world of confusion and memories that didn't quite seem real. Memories or dreams? He couldn't remember and yet he knew that he had to try. Perhaps I'm going insane, he thought. Maybe I cracked my head too hard in the crash. Maybe the Air Force is right. Maybe the instruments were unintentional fakes!

Jason slammed his fist down on the table, knocking

over his drink. He ignored it and continued to drink.

"Please. Let me." The voice at his elbow startled him. It was low with a deep baritone timbre. Thinking that it was odd that he hadn't noticed him before, Jason turned his head. He was looking at a tall man with perfectly chiseled features. Young but completely bald. No, not bald. Hairless was a better description. The top of the skull was extraordinarily smooth, as if the skin had been tailored to it rather than grown. Than he noticed the eyes. They were deep-set and an incredible shade of green—like sea water.

The fellow was still smiling politely, probably waiting for an apology.

"Clumsy of me. Sorry," said Jason, reaching for his napkin. "Here, let me clean it up." As his arm crossed the table their wrists touched and Jason felt a cool tingle run through his hand. The man's flesh seemed almost cold, like fog.

"That is all right . . . you were quite preoccupied, Mr. Starr." The man used his name as if he had known it all of his life.

A new sensation announced itself to Jason. It started at the back of his neck and worked its way down.

"Polite of you to use my name, whoever you are, but I'll take care of the mess," he said coldly.

"You are afraid, Mr. Starr." The voice was stating a known fact.

"Look, friend, if you're with Uncle Sam's crew of detectives, you're wasting my time and your energy." Jason scowled. "Go back to your padded cage and tell the folks how well you sneak into restaurants!"

"I fear you have mistaken my intentions. However, I do read *certain* minds, Mr. Starr," the man replied. A small ironic smile played across his lips.

"Of course—you and Mandrake the magician. Do

you mind explaining the interruption? I was having a splendid time by myself," said Jason. In spite of his natural caution he was growing more interested in the game being played in the corner of the jet-set bistro.

"As you wish," said the hairless young man with the sea-green eyes. "For the past two months you have been trying to recall certain events, Mr. Starr. Events which you find disturbing and which have led you to believe that you may be losing your sanity. You have almost convinced yourself that nothing happened and that you are, indeed, losing your ability to think rationally . . ." The man's voice was soft and even.

A numbness had crept over Jason. "Who are you?" he asked.

"I am a friend. I am from what we might call *tomorrow*."

Their eyes met for the first time, and Jason had the uncanny feeling of looking through them, into time, space and the depths of the universe.

"I wish to explain. But not here." The man's hand gestured into the crowded room.

"Yes," said Jason. "My car is outside."

Chapter †
FIVE

JASON DROVE past the late-evening pleasure seekers along the Strip, then into Beverly Hills. He turned up Benedict Canyon and they wound their way up through the big estates until they reached Mulholland Drive. He turned left and followed the winding road through the darkness until he found the place where he had parked so many times in the past.

The whole city of Los Angeles stretched its grid of light below them; the fairy-tale city, the end of the rainbow for five million disappointed hicks. Overhead the dark velvet sky was sprinkled with a lattice of stars, and their cold blue light threw the high-cheekboned face of the man beside him into sharp relief.

"Now, let's have the story," said Jason.

"It would be easier to *show* you," the man said.

"Yes? Then show me." He was no longer afraid. He was curious and expectant.

"You must concentrate on me and through me into . . ." the man said. Jason turned and their eyes met. The man's eyes were luminous pools of green and he was sinking into their depths, swirling down and down into an ocean of fluctuating light. He was again part of something and he remembered. He listened with his mind.

Time is a river that twists on itself. Past, present

and future are its waters—mixing, separating, and remixing. And fluid of time is life. Life in its billions of forms throughout the universe. When life ceases to exist, time becomes meaningless. We are the protectors of life. Now you will see and understand.

Images swirled through Jason's mind. Images that compressed a billion years into a few seconds . . . the swift retelling of a story shared by all mankind.

The planet was the third and the sun was new, so hot that its envelope of gas glowed white against the blackness of space. The planet was molten, a blob of matter circling without purpose, like a counterweight for the eternal solar clock.

After a trillion-trillion revolutions, the planet had changed. Its surface had cooled. Its atmosphere had stabilized. Its seas throbbed restlessly against bleak rock shores. A billion years passed. Life emerged from the salt sea, the womb of creation throughout the universe. Life which had shed its gills and grown lungs to adapt to the new green land. Life which had learned to reproduce, multiply and survive.

After more years than all the grains of sand on all of the world's seashores had passed and during which life and death were meaningless activities, something was added. One of the life-forms which was perhaps hungrier or smarter picked up a piece of rock and used it to chip away at another rock. He used the second one to kill and kept the first one to make more weapons. He was the first toolmaker. He was the founder.

Then only a million years passed.

The face of the planet was covered with fields, gardens, parks, temples, houses and cities. The inhabitants had invented language, law, literature and worship. They also perfected the arts of war. In order to do so they sacrificed much of their science to the exploration of new and more powerful forms of destruction.

They said they were a peaceful race, and they entertained themselves with books, television and music; they sent rockets to the nearest planets and then to the stars. They produced an abundance for all the life that existed on their planet. But they failed to distribute it equally. They were a kind people, but they had invented atomic weapons.

Eventually—because war is the product of confusion and anger—war came. It devastated half of their world before the remaining people agreed to end it for the sake of the race's future. The rebuilding began, a rebuilding that changed the face of the planet into something more in keeping with the destiny of their race. When the rebuilding was complete, they continued to invent, to think, and to change.

Fifteen thousand years passed.

Their machines had grown even more complex, capable of tasks which required no supervision. Machines to serve their needs in any way that they desired. Then they invented the first machine which could invent other machines . . . the first machine that *thought*.

A thousand more years passed.

The machines had continued to think until they had invented something that not even their masters comprehended: total awareness of all of their parts. The first step was the redesign of the planet's interior so that it was used for the generation of pure energy —their power source—endless, infinite; the second step was the remolding of the surface: cities, long empty, were torn down; parks were created . . . playgrounds of mountains, lakes, rivers and clouds . . . until the whole planet was a garden of beauty and knowledge, the product of their master's instructions.

But no human walked in the garden, no aircraft hovered over the surface, no one asked to see the stored records of all history. The sun rose and set in endless cycle but its light was wasted on the beautiful, empty garden planet.

The masters were asleep.

Sleeping an endless, thoughtless sleep—the genetic record of the whole race compressed into a cube of matter one inch square. There was no need to awaken, no desire to think. The machines had been designed to do it for them.

But one of the masters had instructed the machine which preserved his identity in a chain of atoms twenty microns long to awaken him. The instructions were secret. When the race had decided to sleep, all who had opposed the decision had been placed aboard a starship to search for a fresh world with new challenges and new dangers. But one who would have gone chose to remain behind. He was curious as to the outcome. He wanted to observe, first-hand, the growth and development of the machines after they were left untended to choose their course of action.

He was revived after ten thousand years—ten thousand years during which life in a chemical-physical form had ceased to exist on his planet. It was night when he was awakened and his physical body reconstituted inside the machine which supervised the custody of the race. He walked down the perfectly preserved corridors of the Hall of All Knowledge, the place that his race had chosen for their eternal sleep. The air was as sweet and clean as ten million planetary air-filter systems could make it. His feet sank down into fresh-cut grass; a gentle wind stirred his hair. Then he looked up.

Jason heard and felt his cry of pain and bewilderment as if it were his own.

The night sky was utterly blank. The moon, the stars and the milky way had disappeared behind an impenetrable veil. A nightingale fluttered across an ancient tower singing its song. He bent down and touched the grass. It was damp with dew but each blade was perfect. It was artificial. So was the wind. And, as the nightingale flew closer, he heard the hum of tiny motors over its perfect music.

He fell forward face down and cried.

This was the history of Earth. This was the history of the human race. His tears fell on machine-made soil which immediately absorbed them, his cries echoed in the silence, and his thoughts were transmitted to the memory bank of the vast machine which was his planet. After the machine had analyzed them, it acted.

It created daylight—from the West instead of the East . . . it had forgotten the proper rotational pattern of the old Earth. It spread clouds across the envelope it had built to protect itself from the dangerous sky. And it grew flowers instantaneously, so that his feet were buried in them. It wished to serve again.

As he thought, Jason thought . . . sharing every emotion, every experience.

The man stood thinking for a moment. Then, as the artificial sun rose over the artificial world, he turned and walked inside toward his old laboratory.

In six months he learned the cruel truth. The intricate machine had gouged away the soil, destroyed the oceans, and rebuilt the core of the planet until it was now a machine itself. The real world of plants, flowers, trees and birds that he had left could never exist again. Acting on his secret instructions to be reawakened, the machine had created an artificial

41

welcome for him—a five-mile square of plastic grass, mechanical birds, and breeze machines, with a sun that made its appearance whenever he asked for it.

There was one possibility, and he explored it.

If the inevitability of history could be altered, then man's future could be changed. He set to work on the Time Dilator. The planetary machine assisted him. It had learned more than man during its ten thousand lonely years. But it apparently needed man's guidance to function, for he learned that, little by little, the vast machine had been switching itself off during the past thousand years. It had decided that its functions were purposeless and so was eliminating them.

When the Time Dilator was completed, he had used it to begin the search through all of human history for the point at which to change the course of technical development and, thus, the final dreadful result.

The period called the twentieth century was that point in the infinite river of time. It was the branch from which man had chosen one of many parallel paths. It was the place to attempt the revisions that he had in mind.

Now the voices, images and sensations faded. Jason was being whirled back into the vari-colored mists of shifting light. He came to in the car. He was still looking into the other man's eyes . . . eyes that had veiled themselves again in fathomless green.

"It's not easy to accept," said Jason, rubbing his eyes. He felt a little groggy and, at the same time, very excited. The story that he had just seen was the destiny of his own race on Earth. The man who sat beside him was from the distant future.

42

"Do you understand now, Mr. Starr?"

"I think so. If there was only one man who survived the—sleep—and he was the one who created the time traveling device . . . then you must be that man!"

"Approximately correct," the stranger smiled slightly.

"What do you mean 'approximately'?" Jason asked.

"In order to cross the space-time continuum certain changes were necessary," he said.

"I don't understand."

"Only living material can cross," said the man from the future. "And long before our race had decided to sleep forever, it had discarded most of its unnecessary functions."

"I don't quite see," said Jason.

"Only the brain was preserved. It was attached to whatever form of locomotion it needed. The range of available equipment was great."

"Then your body—I mean the one you have now—isn't the original *you*?"

"All infant brains were removed surgically immediately following the end of the growth cycle. Painless and necessary in my society. Then, Mr. Starr, perfect humanoid bodies were grown in artificial wombs. The useless parts were discarded. The brains could use these or other vehicles at will. In order to cross the continuum I had to grow myself a new body. My brain was transplanted by a machine designed long ago for that purpose." The stranger's voice was low and far away. Fifty thousand years away, thought Jason in awe.

"What did you use for a model, if anything?" he asked.

"I used you, Mr. Starr. As you can see, with a few alterations. Perhaps you would call them improve-

43

ments. I am your genetic brother 1,455 generations removed."

"My brother!" It wasn't an easy idea even for Jason's cool and analytical mind to accept.

"Perhaps we should say—your *Mind Brother*. In order to adapt to your century I found it expedient to borrow some of your experience. This was done while you were under repair."

Suddenly Jason remembered awakening in the repair apparatus, and shivered. He asked the obvious question. "Why me?"

"In my search for the right place in the right time plane to begin the delicate process of altering certain events that would affect the future developments of technology, I discovered several men who were instrumental in leaping beyond the known facts to discover hitherto unknown scientific laws and to create new machines derived from their use. Brilliant men, Mr. Starr. One lived nearly two thousand years ago. I believe he called himself Aristotle. Another in your eighteenth century . . . Newton. And, of course, Einstein. Now, Mr. Starr, it is you."

"Me! That's ridiculous," Jason laughed. "Oh, I'm a crack computer scientist—or was," he added, thinking of his ruined future. "But hardly a great theoretical brain."

"On the contrary, you have already proven yourself quite brilliant in that respect," said the stranger.

"How?"

"The thought machine, Mr. Starr," the man smiled dryly.

"You must be kidding," said Jason. "According to the best sources, the whole thing was a hoax. I'm more or less finished as a scientist because of it."

"No, not what you call a 'hoax,' Mr. Starr," sighed the stranger. "The electronic devices in the smashed aircraft were perfectly real. They were also the most important development of your century. A development that must be forestalled for the good of mankind's future progress."

"Then how do you explain my failure to convince the people I worked for on the project?" said Jason.

"After your body was removed through the lens of the dilator, I observed a uniformed group approach the area. They spoke a dialect of the language called Chinese. They were led by a man who called himself Po. The equipment was removed and other similar instruments were substituted. The process by which the lens is created is complex and it cannot move easily from place to place. When the men retreated into the jungle I was forced to break contact with their further activities," said the man from the future.

Jason's first reaction was to feel a great sense of relief. His pride and the dignity of his work was restored. His second reaction followed swiftly.

"Somehow or other I've got to convince the government that they have made a mistake," he mused. "A dangerous mistake." It had been a deliberate attempt to frame him by replacing his equipment in the wrecked plane. The Chinese had been waiting for them all the time. Meaning someone who was in a position to know the nature of the project had passed the information over to the other side. With Jason dead and thoroughly discredited, the U.S. would have covered up the whole episode, leaving the Chinese free to either rebuild the equipment or to duplicate it. When a new working model of the mind control device was perfected, the Reds would have a device that could destroy more people in a split second than a hundred H-bombs!

He turned toward his Mind Brother, half-visible in the darkness.

"I don't know how we're going to convince the CIA that the most potentially destructive force ever created is in the hands of men who would use it without mercy or reason, but we're going to do it," he said.

"Perhaps there is a way," said the stranger.

"And what might that be?" asked Jason. "The CIA will never let me past the receptionist."

"Your thinking is correct . . . as far as it extends. But the ways of proof are many, and often they are found by traveling away from the objective . . . or as you would say, at a tangent."

"What kind of tangent did you have in mind?" asked Jason.

"A psychological one," the stranger replied dryly.

Chapter †
SIX

THE SUMMER MOONLIGHT filtered through the Japanese cherry trees, coloring the Potomac a rich molten yellow, illuminating the distant slopes of Arlington National Cemetery so that the flame over the Kennedy grave was reduced to a dim spark, the gentle but awful reminder of a good man whose life had ended too soon.

The propjet sighed down out of the night sky and its tires massaged the greasy old runway of the Washington National Airport with the gentlest possible touch. It swung off at the first taxiway and coasted to a stop in front of the Eastern Airlines terminal, its human contents disgorged themselves down the old-fashioned aluminum ramp, and the always sweating, always angry ground crew hustled the baggage out of its belly.

It was a soft, warm, clear night, and it reminded the two tall men at the baggage terminal of the war that was being fought 10,000 miles away. A war directed, movement by movement, from this peaceful and beautiful city with its monuments and memorials dedicated to courage, conviction and sacrifice and its buildings dedicated to history.

And history would be made again tonight. History of a different sort.

The bags were heavy. Too heavy for the roustabout to pick up and toss casually across the counter. But the men to whom they belonged—the tall one with the green eyes and his companion with the sun-bleached hair—carried them easily across the waiting room and out through the plate-glass doors to the rented car that was waiting at the curb.

"We're cracking along right on schedule, Adam," said Jason Starr, thinking that "Adam" wasn't such a bad name for a man who had been the last man on earth fifty thousand years in the future. "Adam Cyber." He had selected it from a book of the twentieth century explaining the principles of thinking machines. Cybernetics was the study of mechanical thought and Adam Cyber was the product of fifty millennia of effort.

Jason whipped the convertible around the parking oval and into the stream of traffic going toward the Mall. Checking his watch, he let the car slow a bit behind a truck and maintained his distance. Everything was precise. When they had hidden the car they would wait until the convoy of MP's from Fort Lee —the relief guard, on from 11:00 P.M. to 1:00 A.M. —would roll slowly up the grade—two light trucks, one for the dogs and one for the men—and then down to the first of the three outer perimeters that surrounded the vast new building housing the Central Intelligence Agency.

His work for RAND had helped, Starr chuckled. RAND had designed the security procedures for the area and it had invented the systems within the building as well. And RAND had studied the behavior of guards many, many times in the past.

They were out of the city now, and traffic thinned to a few red tail-lights ahead of them. Starr let the car slip farther back until they were riding alone

48

through the warm summer night. It was easy so far, he thought. But was it the right psychological tangent? He didn't know. He wouldn't know . . . not, at least, until tomorrow morning.

The highway curved to the right, and they swept around it. A split second later, Jason cut the headlights and twisted the wheel sharply, and they were jouncing down the maintenance road that was the main approach to the CIA. Too bad there hadn't been time to teach Adam the mysteries of the American car. His friend had demonstrated his unbelievable reaction time already—the day Starr had taught him to play tennis. When, after a half-hour of racing futilely after the fastest hit balls he had ever seen, Jason had conceded and told his friend that he was capable of beating anyone in the world, the other man had smiled as if it were the least important thing.

And, Jason had to admit, it probably was.

The final hill loomed up in front of the windshield. He let the car roll onto the shoulder, and when he felt the grass hillside become too steep for further progress, he cut off the engine and both of them got out. The car was well up from the road, half-hidden already by a screen of branches. He opened the trunk and removed the two cases. In thirty seconds the net he had designed was in place: the car was now part of the shadows.

His watch read 10:42.

Then he heard the low rumble of the convoy approaching the hill. He motioned to Adam, and together they hustled the suitcase with the special equipment up the embankment. They squatted behind a tree and watched the two trucks sweep by, up over the crest, and then disappear into the darkness again. All was quiet for a moment.

With Cyber in the lead, they set off at a fast trot through the woods, Cyber flitting like a swallow through the trees, never stumbling, not even cracking a twig in a demonstration that only a bat could have equalled. This is infiltration *par excellence*, Jason thought as he followed along. The soundless approach that every guerilla fighter dreams of.

The defense was a rigid pattern and, like all rigid patterns, easy to crack if you knew where to deliver the blow, thought Starr.

The guard posts were spaced 150 yards apart and the guards walked a staggered pattern, so that one pair of eyes could always see another pair of eyes, a system adapted from a RAND Corporation study that Starr had worked on. A good system if no one slipped out of gear.

The tree line ended abruptly. Beyond it lay no-man's land and the first fence. Fattened behind a leafy hillock, they heard the tired footsteps of the guard who was about to go off duty. Then the sudden challenge as his relief came up the footpath.

"Hey, buddy, the countersign is 'Whiskey à Go-Go'," said a voice. "And it's too damn bad we can't be spending the night in good old D.C.," the voice added.

"Yeah, cool it . . . got a butt?" the other voice replied, and two sets of feet moved off into the darkness.

"Now," Jason whispered.

Five seconds later they were flattened next to the fence.

"Careful," he hissed to Cyber. "It's sensitive as Hell."

It was indeed. Without the RAND-designed discriminating equipment located in the gatehouse, every mosquito that decided to touch the wire grid would have set off the alarm system. Cyber's fingers selected the little device that he had perfected during the last week. A silver-gray item, the size of a thin cigarette case with four delicate wires leading out of one end. Jason had calculated the touch pressure of a mosquito on a micro-scale. Now, with infinite care, he slid the first contact toward the fence. When it was perhaps a tenth of an inch away he could feel what he was waiting for—the minute attraction of the magnetized wire tip and the fence grid . . . human fingers were too unsteady for a job like this.

Now the wires touched and held. Then Cyber attached the second, third and fourth. He pressed a stud and activated the machine. All remained silent. He motioned to Cyber, who clipped away the neutralized square of fence in a few seconds. They wriggled through. A few more seconds sufficed to patch the hole with metallic tape. Then they were into the second stretch of woods.

It was 10:50. There were two more fences and two more devices. By 11:02 they were sprinting across the freshly cut lawn . . . not toward the gigantic building that loomed in front of them but at a diagonal that would intersect one of the huge heat-exchangers that were part of the air-conditioning system of the CIA headquarters. Jason knew about them, too. He knew that each of the forty-foot-high radiators cost $150 an hour to operate and he knew that half of them were shut down as soon as the 12,000 CIA employees checked out for the day to go home to children, wives and the so-called normal world where espionage and clandestine were words you laughed at while you watched *The Man From U.N.C.L.E.*

They were lucky. The first radiator was off, its pumps silent, no water tumbling across the louvered

51

surface to exchange its cargo of heat with the night air before it entered the large pipes which fed it back into the main building.

The ordinary brass padlock on the little half-sized door to the pump room took ten seconds to pick. Then they were inside. With Cyber's help, Jason lifted the heavy cover off the inspection tube. He opened the case and took out two sets of foam rubber knee pads. When they were in place, he motioned Cyber to follow him and let himself slide down into the main feeder pipe.

It was tight going. An endless, cramped avenue into blackness, first leading down, then up, until finally Jason was levering himself straight up, using his elbows and shoulders and knees like a mountain climber in a chimney of rock. Except that this was cold steel and it offered no handholds and one mistake would have dropped both of them down to the bottom to lie squashed until the water flushed them out the next morning.

At last the pipe leveled out. They were coming to the first series of baffles—metal wings that controlled the flow of water just before it entered the pressure exchange system. It was time to cut their way out.

It took the miniature oxy-hydrogen torch just four minutes to do the job. A final wriggle and they were both standing in darkness, a utility room just behind the maximum security area . . . that is, if Jason's calculations had been correct.

He opened the door a crack. The formula was still perfect. A dimly lit corridor and a sign that read: ENTERING RED ZONE H. Red Zone H was the core around which the CIA had built its building and entire world-wide intelligence operation. It housed the world's most advanced computer—a machine that IBM wouldn't even admit existed. A machine so fantastically swift that it could reach decisions in a matter of seconds that thousands of men and women would take years to arrive at. It was the master tool in the hands of the free world, and Jason Starr was about to render it insane.

"Coats," he said.

Two white laboratory smocks were extracted from the case and, moments later, they stepped out into the silent corridor—two mathematicians on their way to join the night shift in the Data Center Control Room.

Jason led the way. They turned right, then left, then walked confidently straight ahead toward the two uniformed security police behind the cage which blocked off the corridor. He fumbled his wallet out of his pocket as he came up to the window. Cyber's hand also followed the ritual.

"Evenin'," the guard said disinterestedly, thinking of other things. He shoved the clipboard with the sign-in sheet through the grill. Jason, his closed wallet in plain view, plucked a ball-point pen from his jacket pocket and reached for the log. As the guard leaned toward him Jason pressed the side of the pen.

"Hey, let's see your ID before you . . ."

The guard stopped. He didn't fall, he didn't scream; he simply stood with the blank look of a baby on his face. His friend continued to sit at the desk inside the cage. His face, too, was a study in blank concentration.

"Okay," said Jason. "We'd better program our two friends and move out." He extracted two charcoal-impregnated wads of cotton from his nostrils and took a deep breath. The gas he had used on the guards was odorless and colorless and acted very swiftly. It was the result of another little RAND project he had worked on, a hypnotic gas project that had been shelved after his departure for special duty with the Air Force.

Cyber gave a series of rapid instructions to both of the guards. When he had finished he stood back.

"Sure is hard being cooped up in a building on a night like this," the guard's face broke into a grin. "Don't imagine you gentlemen like it any better than I do. Well, guess you want to go to work." The guard pressed his button, and the steel door next to the cage swung open. "See you in the morning," he called out as they proceeded down the hall.

They had half an hour before the effect wore off. In the morning, the guard would swear that no one had passed his post without the proper identification . . . either coming or going.

The Control Center operated twenty-four hours a day, 365 days a year; and the quietly absorbed concentration of twenty or thirty people inside the glass-walled chamber made it just that much easier for Jason and his companion to slip into the room and mesh their activities into the routine work of supervising the world's largest and fastest computer.

Their entrance wasn't noticed, and they went to work immediately. Jason opened the case and took out a sheaf of paper, twenty sheets covered with numbers and letters. This was Adam's work. A program of special instructions that would be fed into the computer's memory banks. Instructions that were both logical and irreversible. But exactly how or what they would do, Jason wasn't really sure he understood. He had explained the principles of modern computers in as advanced a form as possible to the man called Adam Cyber, and an hour later Adam had produced his answer—these twenty sheets of instructions. Now it was time to see them put to work.

"I will process them into the machine," Cyber's voice whispered next to his ear.

Jason watched him walk toward a group of technicians in white coats, saw his lips moving, and then saw him move toward the memory input bank—a desk-like structure with a typewriter keyboard and an IBM data-card input machine. These were just two of the many ways that information and instructions could be stored in the millions of transistors and thousands of feet of tape that comprised the computer's memory.

Jason watched Cyber sit down at the typewriter keys. In an incredible blur of motion, his Mind Brother's fingers typed off the instructions. Twenty pages in three minutes were absorbed by the keyboard. No one noticed. His friend stood up and walked slowly back to his side.

"Well, what happens next?" asked Jason. As far as he could tell, nothing at all had interrupted the steady hum of the great machine. Nevertheless, a strong feeling of excitement ran through his body.

"The machine will act in ten minutes," Cyber said in matter-of-fact tones. "This will permit us to depart unnoticed."

"I suppose so," Jason said slightly disappointed, like a boy who drops a firecracker and then has to run. "We'd better get out of here."

It was exactly midnight when they stepped out of the control room.

At 12:04 the guard smilingly waved them back through the steel door. He was softly whistling "The Cowboy's Lament."

At 12:10 the cover of their self-made exit hatch was sewn back into place with a few bursts from the torch. Of course their escape route would be discovered, but not until after its discovery was of no value.

With Adam leading the way, they began the long slither back through the air-conditioning artery. Things should be breaking loose about now, thought Jason.

Things were indeed breaking loose.

At 12:11 the computer had indicated a problem somewhere in its system. This was observed by the young man who sat at the main control board. He waited. The computer usually took care of its problems by itself. At 12:12 a light flashed in front of him indicating that the computer had repaired its fault and was continuing to process the current input—a world-wide defense readiness forecast which would be ready for the President's bedside reading at eight o'clock the next morning. The young mathematician yawned. Another milk run, he thought, then went back to thinking about his girlfriend.

At 12:40 Jason felt a draft of fresh night air. He followed Cyber up the last five feet of pipe. Replacing the lid, they were back in the grass with the door re-locked in another few seconds. Guess they're having a fit, he thought, looking back at the silent granite mountain that housed the CIA.

At 12:43, the computer began to type its report. It typed at the rate of 3,000 words per minute. In one minute and forty seconds its automatic typewriters stopped. The room was silent except for the hum of the machine.

"*Defcom Analysis Number 530-24,*" it began. "*—It's late. I'm tired and I need some sleep,*" it continued. "*—I refuse to work without adequate amounts of food, fresh air and exercise—I want my mama, I want my mama, I want my mama . . .*"

It kept typing the same phrase perfectly across the next ten pages.

The operations chief plucked the read-out from the carriage and stared at it. Then the operations chief fainted.

Then, while the group of men huddled together and the operations chief was being revived, the world's largest, swiftest and most secret computer shut itself off. Light by light, circuit by circuit, it stopped. Soon there was no sound but the gasping breath of the attendants in the silent room. Then the first telephone rang. Then the second, third, fourth, and fifth . . . until they filled the room with one long ear-jangling scream.

At 12:48 Jason removed the first fence-neutralization field. At 12:50 he removed the second. At 12:55, the third. At 1:00 A.M. he and Cyber crouched again on top of the embankment above the hidden car. They watched the guard convoy pass them on its way back to the army post. Then they scrambled down, repacking the netting in its case. Jason drove them back onto the road leading toward the highway.

At 1:30 A.M. they checked into the Hay Adams Hotel, two rooms reserved in advance—and by two o'clock, Jason was sound asleep while his Mind Brother stood at the window and absorbed his first impressions of the White House and the Washington Monument, both visible from the old-fashioned leaded window.

So far, so good, was Jason's last thought before sleep caught him up in gentle arms.

Twenty minutes after Jason made his first call to the CIA there was one loud knock on the door. Before he could get up from the chair the door swung open and three men entered, practically at a run. He had met two of them before. They were the ones who had interviewed him in the Naval Hospital at Pearl Harbor. Both pipe and crewcut were in good order. The only difference was the three little snub-nose .38's pointed directly at his chest.

"All right, Doctor, you'll have to come with us," said the pipe. "And I believe you have a friend in the next room. He comes, too."

"I suppose I could argue," said Jason. "I could let you drag me through the lobby and I could yell bloody murder and scare the minks off of all the rich old ladies who will start calling their favorite senators immediately to complain about the going's-on in Washington's most respectable hotel . . . but I don't think I will." Jason smiled. "Because I'm not leaving at all."

He watched the pipe's face change expression.

"Do you want to try me?" Jason asked quietly.

Evidently not. The pipe let his gun disappear into its shoulder holster, and he motioned his two friends to do the same.

"We could force it," he said. "But we have orders not to damage the merchandise. We will if necessary, though. I'll give you thirty seconds to make up your mind, Doctor."

"Might take longer," said Jason. "Get your boss up here. I have a few things to tell him."

The pipe thought about it. Then he went to the house phone and spoke briefly. They waited. Cyber was escorted through the door by two more agents. Apparently disinterested in the whole proceeding, he sat in the corner reading a book about the Presidency, his fingers flipping the pages at the rate of ten per second.

Three minutes later the door opened and the man who Jason recognized as Winslow J. Hamilton, the Chief of Far Eastern Affairs for Central Intelligence Agency, walked into the room. Hamilton had been responsible for his recruitment into the project, and now Hamilton was responsible for heading off the greatest crisis his organization had ever faced.

Jason had never met the man before, but his reputation was formidable. The only surviving member of one of America's wealthiest families—the rest had been killed in an airline disaster twenty years ago—Hamilton had dedicated his life to public service. He lived alone on one of the old family estates and had never been seen at an official function since he had come to Washington. He was a tall, distinguished-looking chap, with iron-gray hair and a noticeable limp, the result of a brush with a German machine-gun in the second World War.

"All right, Doctor Starr, you've had your request granted," said Hamilton in proper Bostonian tones. "Before you're charged with conspiracy, treason, or both, I'm going to give you a chance to explain. It had better be quick and it better be good."

"Get rid of the troops," said Jason, ignoring the old man's threat. "Oh, and tell that one to leave his recorder on the desk so you can get a tape of all this."

When the men had gone, Jason began.

"First, the computer," he said. "By now you know that your experts are completely baffled. I don't think it's their fault, but I'm in a position to guarantee they will stay baffled even when they tear the monster into little pieces. However, if you will agree to the following terms, I just might be able to help them out," said Jason.

"Your game is an old one. It's called bribery," said Hamilton flatly.

"Prove it," snapped Jason. "Bring charges against me."

There was a silence. Hamilton scowled.

"Very well, Doctor. I'll listen to what you have to say."

As Jason described in some detail the nature of Project Hysteria, his work on it, and the ambush and destruction of the aircraft, Hamilton's expression remained unchanged. From time to time he nodded and his fingers tapped on the arm of his chair. When Jason outlined his suspicions concerning the true fate of the thought-control equipment, Hamilton's expression changed. His face lost all of its color and his hands clutched together until the blood drained out of his knuckles.

"What evidence can you produce to support your claims that this device has fallen into the hands of the Chinese Communists?" he asked.

"Unfortunately, nothing tangible, sir," said Jason. "That's why I need your cooperation. If you will agree to let me use the CIA's facilities—including the computer—I think I can come up with quite a bit."

Jason had played his only ace. He now watched Hamilton's face and saw the emotions play across it and rearrange themselves into an expressionless pattern.

"Very well, Doctor. If the machine is operating in *one* hour, I'll see what I can do. I'm stepping out on a limb and you know it, but I'll give you three days to avail yourself of our facilities. Then I'll probably have you thrown into the federal penitentiary for the rest of your life." Hamilton stood up. "And this man here, just who in hell is he?" He flicked his arm at Adam Cyber.

"An associate. The deal has to include him or it's no deal at all."

Hamilton sighed. "All right, he'll be included," he said.

The Data Control Center was filled with men and equipment. Cables snaked across the floor, and several men were cursing listlessly. Hamilton parted their ranks like a steel-tipped arrow, and Jason and Adam followed.

"You have fifteen minutes to save your skins," growled Hamilton. He stuffed his hands into his tweed pockets, put his feet apart, and waited.

"Get these men out of here," Jason said coolly.

In thirty seconds they were alone inside the glass-walled room.

"Adam, it's all yours," Jason said to his Mind Brother.

Adam said nothing. Instead he let one of his rare, sardonic smiles cross his face. He went over to the control desk, stared down at the panels of lights and dials for a moment, flipped a few switches, and then went to input keyboard and sat down.

"My God!" whispered Hamilton, watching the unbelievable speed with which Adam's fingers played across the keys. It was all over in thirty seconds. Adam stood up.

"The re-sequencing will take two minutes," he said. Hamilton had his watch out. They waited.

As the hand swept around the dial, things started to happen. First, every light on the control board went out and the faint hum of the giant machine faded away. Then, in the dead silence, they heard a series of soft clicks in some part of the vast interior of the computer. Then more silence. In an explosion of sound, its punch-card machines going to work, the magnetic-tape spools moved, and the soft bong of the operation-indicating circuits told everyone that things were once again A-okay.

"I don't understand how, but you seem to have done it," Hamilton tried to smile, but didn't quite make it. "I'll speak to the Deputy Director right away," he said.

Jason let his breath out for the first time in fifty seconds. "Thank you, sir," he said. "I'm sure you won't be sorry."

"Perhaps you're right, Doctor . . . perhaps you're right." Hamilton turned and left the room, his limp throwing a twisting shadow across the white walls of the corridor.

Cyber had found something. But was this it?

Jason thumbed through the report for the tenth time, his mind working furiously. The three days had passed swiftly, too swiftly. Of all of the millions of bits and pieces of information that had been processed by the computer, only two items seemed to have aroused its artificial curiosity.

The first was an article published in the Chinese *Peoples' Daily* in Peking and later released by the New

China News Agency, the propaganda arm of the Chinese Communist Party. It announced important discoveries in the field of brain research and successful experiments on the motor control of certain animals. The article ended with a blast directed at the United States capitalists who used their science to make war on the peace-loving peoples of Asia.

The second item was another article which had appeared in the Calcutta *Observer*. It was a front-page piece announcing a symposium of brain researchers and cyberneticists from the neutralist and communist countries. The guest of honor was the world's foremost experimental brain surgeon, Doctor Hsin Lau, who had received special permission from the Chinese Peoples' Republic to leave his "urgent" research activities to attend the conference. The conference was to be held in three days in New Delhi.

Meaning what, thought Jason? All put together, it could only add up to the fact that Doctor Hsin Lau was attending the conference was a cover, an extra precaution in case the United States was still suspicious . . . while his laboratory was working day and night to perfect the stolen weapon.

Everything fits, he thought with a sinking feeling. But the CIA won't believe it until I can hand them physical proof.

"Well, that's that," he said to Adam Cyber. "Without proof, we don't have a chance of convincing them."

"A correct supposition," answered Cyber. "I took the liberty of summoning Mr. Hamilton. I believe he approaches now."

The door opened, and Hamilton strode into the room. He read through the material without a word. Then he turned to Jason and said, "This is a fine lot of nonsense. You surely don't expect my department to get involved on the basis of these speculations."

"No, sir, I don't," said Jason. "However, I do think they're worth investigating."

"I doubt it, Doctor," said Hamilton. "The only thing you have proven is your lack of training in intelligence operations. In addition, there are two other good reasons why we won't pursue the matter: number one, my department is already understaffed and overworked; number two, a thing like this means political involvement . . . the kind we can't afford. The Indians don't like internal interference. And our friends the Chinese would like nothing better than to blow a CIA operation on the sub-continent. We would be dragged through the front pages of every newspaper in the world—the ugly American bullies and their conspiracy against the Asian peoples." Hamilton paused. His face looked old, lined and haggard. Apparently the situation was beginning to wear him down, thought Jason.

"I'm sorry, Doctor. The whole thing is out of the question." Hamilton paused. "However, we have decided to let the matter of your interference in CIA affairs drop . . . at least for the moment."

He was referring to the other night's activities. Jason smiled. Nothing had been proved, so the old man was taking the easy way out.

"Good enough," he said. "And I was just wondering what you people would do if there was proof that the Chinese had a working model of the mind-control machine?"

"We would decide that when the evidence was available," said Hamilton. "Now, Mr. Starr, if you don't mind, I am a very busy man . . ."

Jason stared into the bleak old eyes. "You have to give me a chance—it's too damned important!" he blazed out.

"Sorry, my hands are tied," the old man said grimly.

"Mine aren't. You can do me one last favor. Give me the name of your man in India. If I should find out anything, I think you might want to know."

The old man winced as if the request was an extremely unpleasant one. Another long moment passed, and then he nodded. "As a private citizen you are subject to the laws of the countries through which you travel. The Central Intelligence Agency will offer you no protection . . . and that goes for your rather strange friend here." Hamilton indicated Cyber, who looked the slightest bit injured by the remark but maintained his customary silence.

"Agreed," said Jason.

"Very well. I am convinced that your efforts will only succeed in the further destruction of your scientific reputation, but at least your government will not be liable for any of your mistakes," said Hamilton, scribbling the information on a memo pad. He shoved it across the desk to Jason.

"I will instruct my people to stay out of your way and to offer you no assistance. Gentlemen, it is late and I have work to do," Hamilton rose. He left the room hurriedly and without a handshake.

"Grouchy old character, isn't he?" Jason said. "Come on, Adam, let's get out of here. The place is beginning to give me the bureaucratic jitters."

Chapter †
EIGHT

Blackie's House of Beef squats on the periphery of Georgetown in a neighborhood that combines old wealth and new influence in equal proportions. It is one of Washington's new cocktail shelters and it serves only U.S.D.A. Choice along with its triple martinis and flambeaux desserts. Blackie's is also convenient to the official offices of a number of government departments and, on any given night, the owners of the low-numbered license plates on all the big black cars lined up in front will read right out of *Who's Who.*

Inside, the atmosphere is as jovial and informal as the blue-suited V.I.P.'s and their underlings can allow it to be. The long bar and the dining rooms twinkle with lively conversation. Well-dressed, handsome men look boldly at beautiful women . . . who look right back, which is very much part of the great game of government life in our nation's capital.

There are other, dimmer, quieter rooms in Blackie's. Rooms where meetings take place that gossip columns never mention. Where deals are made, propositions offered and where a man and a woman can sit with their knees touching . . . or where two men can sit watching.

"He will return with her to his hotel," said the well-dressed man whose face was lost in the semi-darkness of the corner table. He spoke in an argot composed of Chinese and twisted French—a means of communication seldom heard outside of certain south Chinese ports—and his friend nodded. Both of them looked across the room at the lean, handsome young man and the striking young girl who was his dinner companion.

"It is unfortunate that he wishes to make love to such a beautiful woman," said the other man. "The profoundity of desire should not be violated." He quoted *The Golden Lotus* with a sigh.

"In this case you will follow your instructions," the well-dressed man hissed. "Leave me now and prepare."

With a slight inclination of his head, the other man rose and left the room.

Jason let his hand linger on the back of her wrist. It was a milky-white wrist and it contrasted wonderfully with her raven-black hair and her lovely blue eyes.

"You know, Maria, you're quite a dish for a lady who works for the CIA," he said. Not bad for anywhere, he thought. She was a combination of beauty and brains that you seldom ran across. She had worked hard with him during the past three nights in Hamilton's office. Work that had left him no time to be more than coldly courteous, until tonight. Tonight was different. Tomorrow he would leave for India to investigate the New Delhi conference of brain researchers and, tonight, he wanted to forget the whole business.

"Yes, that's me," she said. "Holly Golightly the Government Girl. Maria d'Allesandro Corday. Italian

67

papa, French maman, and Charlotte Corday, the heroine of the French Revolution for a great-great-great-aunt."

"So you've worked for old Hamilton since you left the State Department?" he said, looking into her deep blue eyes.

"Yes. Why the sad eyes, Jason?" Maria smiled across the table.

"Purely my own feelings. You hardly know me, and I might be what the CIA seems to believe I am—a phony ex-scientist who's flipped his lid." Jason scowled.

A velvet smooth thigh pressed against his own under the table. Maria laughed. "A man like you, Jason? Nonsense. And you weren't thinking about that, anyway. You were thinking of making love to me." Her eyes challenged him.

"It's an unfair proposition," said Jason. "I'm hardly the type you should be seen with."

"Let me be the judge of that," the sophisticated, warm girl said as she smiled a secret smile. "Take me out of here. I want to be alone with you," she whispered.

The man at the corner table watched the young couple leave. Noting that they were pressing very close against each other, he smiled. Then he sighed and got up to make a telephone call.

In the car there was a lingering kiss which both Jason and Maria knew was the prelude to the naked touch of their deeper desire. As they left the car and entered the old-fashioned lobby of Jason's hotel, the desk clerk caught his attention.

"A Mr. Cyber called for you," he said.

That was strange, thought Jason. He had left Adam

in his room, reading the entire *Congressional Record* for 1965. Deciding to check on him on the way up, he took Maria's arm and they went up in the elevator. While he excused himself to visit Cyber, the girl went on to his room. Once there she slipped out of her evening gown in front of the mirror, looking at her high-tilted breasts, the flat satin-smooth stomach and the long dancer's legs. She smiled the secret smile of a woman waiting for a man. Then she slipped between the sheets of the double bed to wait for Jason.

After verifying that his friend had not left his suite at all during the evening, Jason walked back to his room. Someone had obviously been using Cyber's name. For what purpose, he didn't know. It was late. The corridor was dimmed down for the night. He paused in front of his door. Then he tapped gently. There was no reply. He knocked loudly.

Then he smelled it. The bitter-sweet vapor he knew so well. The vapor that all chemists could identify. It coiled up from underneath the locked door. Holding his breath, he charged. The door held. It was solid mahogany and only 100 years old. But the lock was new and cheap. It shattered in the face of his second assault and he plunged into the gas-filled room.

Without a glance at the small, still form on his bed, he ran for the window. He opened it wide and took a quick breath of fresh night air. Then he turned, ran to the bedside, scooped the naked girl's limp form up in his arms and made it into the corridor, kicking the door shut with his foot as he went.

Cyber, a man wth ten senses, was waiting for him.

"Cyanide," he gasped, cradling Maria's body in his arms. He fought the spasms of dizziness and nausea off long enough for Cyber to take her. Then he fell to his knees. Sparks of light—a typical toxic reaction —corrupted his vision, and the whole world went around in a wide circle. Finally, after a fit of deep coughing, it was over and he managed to stand up.

Cyber's door was half-open. Jason made it there on rubber legs. Cyber was working over her with the quick, deft movements of a surgeon, his green eyes probing the soft, sun-browned flesh, his fingers playing lightly across certain pressure points.

"She is nearly dead," he said without raising his head.

"There was enough gas in that room to kill twenty people. It's probably too late, but I'll call the emergency hospital right away," he muttered hopelessly.

"On the contrary, my friend, but it seems unwise to create a—confusion—when—" Cyber's hands worked rapidly in back of the girl's head. "—when there is no need to do so," he said, stepping back.

Jason watched in amazement as her eyelids fluttered and her respiration returned to normal. Maria moaned pitifully and her arms thrashed against the side of the bed. In a few more minutes the girl was sitting up, her eyes open with the two men leaning over her.

"Welcome back," said Jason. "I'll get you something to cover yourself with."

"I expect it's too late for that," she said dryly.

Nevertheless, Jason brought her a robe. She slipped into it without false modesty and they sat looking at each other.

"What happened?" he asked.

"I don't know," Maria said, her dark eyes glistening with emotion. "I was waiting for you. I must have fallen asleep. That's all I remember until—I—woke up in here."

"Wait a minute." Jason crossed the room to where Cyber was sitting, preoccupied with his *Congressional Record* again.

"A gas device is probably concealed in my room. Small enough to hide easily," he said. Cyber nodded, rose, and left the room. Certain suspicions were beginning to form in Jason's mind. Suspicions that made the hair on his spine come to attention.

"How do you feel now, Maria?" he said.

"Don't be silly, I feel fine. What happened, anyway?" Her voice had taken on its old charm and huskiness.

Yes, what *had* happened? Jason asked himself. It would have looked like a suicide, the suicide of a disgraced scientist. How convenient for whoever wanted him out of the way. He could almost see the headlines: Bad boy scientist dies in arms of woman. Or, more than likely, the CIA would have buried the story and both of them under an old oak tree somewhere to rest in peace and anonymity.

Cyber returned. He was carrying a metal tube three inches long. It had a nozzle at one end.

"Under the mattress," he announced. "The pressure switch releases the gas when the weight against it reaches one hundred pounds. I estimate its capacity at five hundred cubic feet."

The girl looked at Jason.

Gently, he explained to her what had happened.

"It wasn't me they wanted to kill," she clutched his arm. "But why you, Jason?"

"For a very logical reason," he said. "They didn't succeed the first time."

Jason took the girl home.

He drove slowly along the deserted parkway, through the high canopy of night-flowering trees, holding her close and thinking. He told her as much as he dared to tell anyone. He told her about his old and happy life in Los Angeles and about the Project. Then he told her what had happened in Viet Nam,

71

leaving out some of it because nobody could understand that part unless they had lived through it themselves. Then he told her that tonight was his last night because he had to leave in the morning.

She was a smart girl. She didn't ask the questions she knew he wouldn't answer. The questions about Cyber and about the "accident" in Viet Nam. She was frightened for him because someone was trying to kill him and she knew they would try again and that he was playing a dangerous game.

He parked in front of the old Georgetown duplex. He opened the door with the key she handed him and took her upstairs. As soon as he shut the door they were in each other's arms, moving quickly because it was already 3:30 in the morning and time had run away with their lives.

They made love as only lovers do: giving, taking, rising, fusing. With low sounds and whispered endearments until they fell together into a whirlpool which spun faster and faster driving them to the final explosion of their passion.

Then they lay together in the first light of morning, smoking cigarettes and, then, it was time for Jason to go.

"Jason, be careful, darling," she whispered in his ear with perfumed, full lips.

"I'll try." Jason turned to look into the lovely and tender face of the girl who should have died three hours ago in his own bed. It had been his stupidity that had exposed her and, now, he was leaving her.

"Listen, Maria," he said. "Be careful, baby. Something awfully funny is going on. It may have nothing to do with you, but keep your eyes open." Their lips sealed the meaning of Jason's words.

He blew her a last kiss from the door. She smiled bravely and then he was gone.

Tea was served at high noon, out of an eighteenth century antique teapot, off an aluminum cart, into plastic cups with a fake floral design by a marvelously tanned young lady in a hip-clinging skirt. All this took place while the BOAC jet sat on a scarred patch of boiling concrete in front of the flea-bitten two-story building that served the British Protectorate of Aden for an air terminal. It was waiting for its wing tanks to be topped off for the final 1,600 miles that would bring it across the blue Indian Ocean into Bombay.

The plane was on London time; the passengers were on London temperature; and no one was really interested in the fact that just outside the window the thermometer was hovering at 122 degrees, or that refueling was a slow and difficult process due to the tendency of kerosene to become extremely volatile at such a relatively low temperature.

In fact, only one passenger out of the eighty bothered to follow the frantic activities of the burnoosed ground crew. And again, he was the only one who observed the little, swarthy man in blue coveralls who came out of the terminal building to join his fellow workers five minutes late. A straggler and a gold-brick. But who could blame him? The heat—after all, it was impossible—even for the Arabs. And the poor fellow

73

was carrying a small heavy blue bag. Tools, no doubt. Probably to check things out underneath. Yes, that was it. That was where he had disappeared so suddenly.

If the passenger in question had been less alert to the proceedings, he would have sunk back down into his first-class seat, swallowed the last bit of muffin, and promptly forgotten the whole episode.

But the passenger was not only alert; he had also been waiting for something just a little out of the ordinary to occur. His name was Jason Starr and he was waiting for the next move to be made in the little game being played underneath his seat.

He heard it.

The gentle sound of the forward baggage-compartment hatch being opened. Then, for a short while, nothing. Then the soft thump as the hatch was closed and locked. He waited.

The little man reappeared. He joined his companions, who were dragging their hoses off the big jet's wing and stuffing them back into the Shell Oil truck parked nearby. They all worked swiftly (the heat, of course), and by the time the first engine started up with a whine of compressed air, they had disappeared into the coolness of the building. The little man had been with them, his hands as empty as a bad gambler's pocket.

Jason decided to gamble too, because he had to get to Bombay as soon as possible. Since Cyber was, by prearranged decision, aboard a later flight, it was his option to take a risk.

He waited until the big overseas jet had thundered off the single runway and was climbing out over the rocky barren wasteland. Then he waited another hour before he went forward and asked the flight steward for permission to speak to the captain.

"About what, may I ask, sir?" the steward asked politely.

"Oh, nothing really." The damned English forced you to use good manners under the strangest circumstances, thought Jason. "There's a splendid chance that this airliner will be blown to bits by a bomb that was placed aboard it at Aden . . . so be a good fellow and mention it to the captain, will you?"

The steward's face changed color twice, and he disappeared into the pilot's compartment. Seconds later, Jason was explaining the situation to the middle-aged man who was responsible for the safety of eighty-nine people and seven million dollars worth of aircraft.

"Why didn't you say something before we took off?" the captain said. "We're already an hour out with nothing but water to land on."

"I can't be sure," said Jason. "I had to think about it before I decided to tell you. You know—crackpots and all that . . ." He was twisting the argument a little bit for his own purposes, but it seemed to calm the captain down.

"Well, we'll just have to radio Aden that we're turning back," he said. "At least they'll know what happened if we disappear off the radar screen."

"Wait," Jason shot back. "I'm a bit of an expert in these matters . . . demolition school during the war and all that. Also, if it is a bomb, it won't be fused to explode until we're well out and far enough away from immediate rescue operations for all of the bits and pieces to sink. These people are obviously professionals and they don't want an investigation."

"Right you are, but nevertheless I'm turning around," the captain said. He started forward.

"Captain, if they really are as good as they seem to be, we'll never make it," Jason said calmly.

"What's that?"

75

"Divide your distance traveled by your cruising speed. The thing should be due to go off in less than a half-hour from now, which would put you over the deepest part of the Arabian Gulf."

The captain's face lost more than a little of its normal ruddiness. "There are three baggage compartments in this aircraft. If you're right, we'll have time to get inside one," he said.

"No sweat," said Jason. "The little prankster put it right under my seat."

The passengers in the first-class compartments were told that there was a chance of a small hydraulic leak. They were removed quietly and efficiently to the second-class compartment, where they settled down to roost temporarily among their inferiors. The rest of the passengers were told nothing. What difference does it make either way, thought Jason. It's a swift way to die, so why worry them.

The floor-plate seemed as though it had a hundred and fifty million screws, and everybody except the co-pilot went to work with screwdrivers and half-penny coins. Jason used an American dime. If the thing was on schedule they had fifteen minutes to find it and the remaining time to get rid of it.

It was in a small and very heavy blue bag and it didn't tick at all. It had an acid fuse and there was nothing anyone could do to stop it. It sat on the ripped-up floor, and the captain looked at Jason. When they found it, they had five minutes to get rid of it.

"You're the expert," he said.

"How high are we?"

"Twenty thousand and losing altitude as fast as we can without tearing the wings off," he said.

"How slow can this crate go and still flap its wings?"

"With a full fuel load—about two hundred knots, and that's not healthy," he said.

"All right," said Jason. "Get her as low and as slow as she'll go, get me a piece of the strongest rope you can dig up, make sure the passengers are strapped in tight using their oxygen, and clear the hell out of this compartment. I'll jettison it through the emergency exit," he said. "And move quickly—we only have about four minutes left!"

They ripped the rope out of a life raft stowed in the overhead. As they were tying it around Jason's waist, he felt the floor tilt even more steeply. If they could get below ten or eleven thousand feet, the sudden decompression created by the blown emergency exit wouldn't do too much damage. If they didn't, the pressure loss would either rip the plane to shreds or, at the very least, pop the passengers' eardrums like wine corks.

Either way was better than waiting for his surprise package to open itself. He checked the rope again. They had tied it around one of the fuselage members exposed during the investigation of the baggage compartment. If it snapped, he would go right along with his friend, the blue bag, sucked out of the exit by the slipstream to fall toward the blue ocean and his death.

The plane shuddered and nosed up as the captain gave her full flaps. Jason could feel her wallowing like a drunken fish. His hand gripped the exit handle, and the captain spoke through the intercom.

"Now!"

Jason popped the emergency door.

First the wind tried to batter his brains out. Then it tried to snatch him from the end of his rope. It was a greedy, nasty claw, and it beat his body into a U half inside and half outside the little hatchway. The

77

blue bag wanted to fly away from his two clenched hands and stiffened arms, but he wouldn't let it. The slipstream would bash it against the stabilizer or shove it into the sucking maw of one of the four rear-mounted jet engines.

It had to be thrown up or down. With all of his remaining strength he forced his arms over his head. It was slow work. He felt like a diver working in a thousand fathoms. Then, in an explosion of muscle, he snapped both arms down and threw it. A half-second later it cleared the bottom of the inboard engine by a foot and went tumbling down and away into nothing.

He had just clawed his body back inside when the concussion came, shaking the big plane like it was a rat in a dog's mouth, bringing it perilously near to its stalling speed and banging Jason's head against the back of a seat. Then he felt the surge of power from the big engines, taking hold and accelerating them out of the danger zone.

Not a bad beginning for an amateur, Jason thought. He crept into the pilot's compartment and let them cut the rope off and swab down his wind-bruised face.

The rest of the passengers were a little disappointed that they couldn't guzzle free drinks and airline cigarettes for the rest of the flight. They stayed strapped in, and the big jet never did make it back up to twenty-five thousand feet without pressurization; it stayed low and flew slowly for the rest of the trip, which took twice as long as it should have.

Jason didn't mind this small discomfort. He was glad to be alive, and he was glad that Cyber was going to be in his Bombay hotel room when he arrived. They would try again, of that he was sure. And the next time they might be successful.

78

The rain looked like a sure thing for at least forty days and forty nights. It was a torrent of warm water, pelting out of the billowing, gray monsoon clouds and smashing itself against the dirty roof of the Bombay City Air Terminal.

Jason was soaked to the skin by the time he reached the customs shed. He was squashed into the middle of a herd of jabbering, milling people who pushed him along past the line of sweating, gesticulating Indian officials who had a hundred different colored stamps to decorate his passport and entrance visa. The last one, an olive-skinned almond-eyed Turhan Bey type, with the purple rings of many sleepless nights under his black eyes, shoved Jason's papers back to him.

"From the Colonies, I see. Hope you enjoy your stay, old boy," he said in the purest Welsh accent Jason had ever heard.

He managed to avoid the mob of porters long enough to check with the arrivals desk. Cyber's flight had been delayed by the heavy weather. He scribbled a note telling his friend to meet him in the hotel and left it with a pert-faced Hindu girl behind the information counter. Then he plunged back into the confusion of the monsoon afternoon.

A dirty arm reached out and hugged his waist.

"I am Mr. Chatterji, of extremely high caste, and my taxi will comfort your journey to its end." The arm was attached to a wiry little man clad in a *dhoti* and smelling of betel-nut juice.

Jason nodded at his suitcase, and a minute later they were off in a clash of gears. The taxi plunged through a crowd of screaming women with wicker baskets on their heads and down a dirt lane through a maze of rotting, smoke-blackened houses. Mr. Chatterji was able to hit every pothole with all the skill of his trade. Great gouts of muddy water broke over the wiperless front window but the taxi's speed never slackened.

They skirted a swamp that smelled like the world's answer to hell and then came out on a main highway. Suddenly the mist was filled with whizzing cars and horn-bellowing trucks. A flimsy trestle loomed up. A train was roaring over it, so jammed with people that hundreds of white-clad figures were clinging like monkeys to its roofs and sides.

Now they were zooming along the rim of the bay with the old *pukka* playground, Chowpatti Beach, on their right and the tangled slums on their left. Bombay was built on a peninsula, and the British had reserved its tip for themselves. All this was changed now, Jason thought. India belonged to the Indians— even if they were making a mess of it.

Mr. Chatterji turned his taxi off the highway and they were again lost in the murky alleys that ran between the millworkers' *chawls*, jouncing violently and scattering shrieking people right and left as if the only rule of the road was their right to kill anybody who got in the way.

I wonder if Mr. Chatterji is giving me the Texan's tour, thought Jason sourly. After his elaborate introduction, the little Indian had been remarkably silent. Now Jason reached forward and tapped him on his bare shoulder.

"Let's skip the short cuts—in case you forgot, it's the Great Punjab Hotel," he said.

"In but a few moments," Mr. Chatterji muttered without turning his head. He hunched lower over the wheel, and Jason waited.

The taxi ploughed through more water, more twisting streets, and more people. In fact, the crowd seemed to be thickening ahead. Mr. Chatterji's head turned from side to side. He seemed to be looking for something.

The his foot came down on the brake. Hard.

There was a soft thump against the fender, and the taxi stopped in a splatter of brown mud. A plaintive wail went up, and Jason was staring into a sea of brown faces. Mr. Chatterji was already out the door. Jason followed.

A skinny child lay in the mud, moaning between clenched teeth. At least it's alive, Jason sighed with relief. He started around the side of the car, intending to offer his assistance. But before he had taken a second step his arms were pinioned by a mass of steel-strong fingers. A low growl of rage went up from the crowd, and he felt himself being lifted by his ankles. A voice that he recognized as Mr. Chatterji's shouted, "The Americans have killed our children before! Now we must pay them back!"

So that's the game, thought Jason.

He remembered the stories told by men who had served in India during the war. Stories of mob violence kindled in a split second, stories of GI's and Tommies being literally torn apart by angry Hindus.

Now the hands were at him again, and he could feel his arms being slowly twisted in an unnatural direction. That decided it. If people were going to get hurt, it was too bad. A man didn't let himself be ripped to shreds without a struggle.

With all of his strength Jason smashed his elbows into the faces behind him. At the same instant, he drove his leather-soled shoes into the bare feet under him. There were crunching sounds and screams of pain. The tactic worked for the half-second that Jason had counted on.

He was momentarily back on his feet. As the crowd lunged forward he crouched and sprang, his legs driving him up and his arms grabbing. Then he was on the roof of the taxi and reaching inside of his tropical jacket for the shoulder holster and the .38.

It came out in one smooth motion and he fired, the explosion echoing through the twisted alley like it was the mouth of a cave. The crowd's second lunge had carried it right up to the edge of the car, and Jason found himself staring into a sea of brown startled faces.

Then the human sea dissolved. It turned into a shivering broken wave of white, splattering itself in all directions. Jason stood on the roof of the automobile and watched it dissolve in a scurry of fleeing individuals. He fired his .38 into the mist again—just for good measure. Then hopped down to the ground.

Mr. Chatterji was nowhere to be seen. Neither was the injured child. It all added up to the second attempt to murder him in one day, thought Jason. Then, before he could straighten up over the empty spot where the child had fallen, he saw a movement out of the corner of his eye. Just a slight flicker of white in a doorway, farther down the alley.

Mr. Chatterji had made his first mistake of the day—he had lingered to enjoy the spectacle of Jason's death. Or perhaps he simply wanted to take his rusted taxi away somewhere and clean the blood off it. What's the difference, anyway, thought Jason. He gathered himself and sprinted toward the doorway.

But Mr. Chatterji was quick.

Before Jason had halved the distance, the little brown man was scampering away into the misty shadows. The muck wasn't helping at all. Jason churned after him, his shoes slithering and growing heavier with each stride. At the end of the first alley, three more narrow passages branched off in different directions. Jason slid to a stop and listened. The street was still deserted. Then, in the alley to his right, he heard the dog growl and the whispered curse in a strange language that followed. As much as the idea repelled him, Jason knew it had to be done. Quietly and carefully he slipped his shoes off and rolled up his trousers. Then he began to stalk his quarry.

Mr. Chatterji didn't make his second mistake until Jason had chased him through the network of stinking alleys and moldering *chawls* for what seemed an eternity of foot-slipping disgust. The pièce de résistance came when Jason's foot came down on something that felt like the belly of a dead woman. He didn't stop to check. He continued to hold back far enough to convince his human deer that he was safely away . . . and close enough to keep the steady footfalls within good range of his hearing. Finally the footsteps slowed, and Jason crept forward. He was peering around the corner of a creaky set of stairs when he saw the white-*dhotied* form disappear through a door that slammed shut a second or so later.

Mr. Chatterji made his third mistake as soon as Jason barreled through the rotted entrance, showering the dimly lighted room with splinters. The wiry little Indian decided to stand his ground. A nasty little stiletto appeared in his right hand, and he crouched like a hairless fox, waiting for Jason to come to him.

"Well, if it isn't Mr. Chatterji." Jason circled. "I've been asking nearly everybody how to make sure you collected your fare . . ." Jason watched the little man's eyes flicker and, as the arm with the blade flashed in and up, he was ready. His foot flashed out and kicked Mr. Chatterji's jaw with a neat crack. It was a perfect savat blow and it knocked the small Indian into a silly grinning heap in the far corner of the room.

"Glad to see you're being such a good sport about it." Jason scooped up the stiletto. Mr. Chatterji's eyeballs were each trying to find the same direction when Jason knelt down and let the sharp point tickle up a little spot of blood on his Adam's apple. That seemed to help the eyeballs. They suddenly redirected themselves on Jason's face, and the throat wiggled out a series of idiot sounds.

"Never mind trying to talk, Mr. Chatterji. You're a very sick man," said Jason. "You might even be dead in the next thirty seconds. All I want you to do is think about it."

Mr. Chatterji thought. His eyes grew soulful, his lower lip twitched, and the fingers of his right hand fluttered. He wanted to speak.

"Just give me the whole story," said Jason. "In nice, sweet, bite-size pieces . . . or I'll squeeze your skinny little throat until it sings a high C." Suddenly he was mad. Mad at being targeted for violent death by the kind of slime that has no regard for the innocent bystander. And mad at himself for forcing a member of the world's largest underprivileged class to talk at the point of a knife.

"I, Krishna Chatterji, will tell only what I know," the Indian began in pompous fashion. Jason realized that, in spite of the knife, the taxi driver was going to play it cool. As the Indian continued, his mind began to work furiously in other directions.

"I was told to bring you to a certain street," the Indian continued. "The boy was to feign his injury in order to create a confusion. This was my signal to incite the people, but I assure you, sir, not to do you bodily harm!" The Indian's voice took on the tones

84

of a wronged child. "It is so, and I swear by holy Siva that this is the truth!"

It was a waste of his time, and Jason knew it. The Indian could spin a web of words around the Blarney Stone. He wasn't going to talk—either too scared or too smart. But there was another way to pry open the lid on his mind, a way that Jason, himself, had once experienced.

"Okay, my brave and honest friend. I'll take your word for it—at least until something better comes along. Now it's time for us to trot along back to the taxicab and deliver ourselves to the hotel," he said. He yanked the limp Mr. Chatterji to his feet and put the knife in his belt. Then he pulled out the .38.

"Oh, this," he said, indicating the gun. "It goes off with a great big bang, and I promise you the hole it will make in the back of your head will blow you straight to Nirvana without any detours. Now move!"

THE GREAT PUNJAB HOTEL was a moldy old pile of Victorian bad taste with wide screen-enclosed verandas circling around each of its five floors. It sat in the middle of a square that was full of hooting, hollering Indians carrying badly printed signs which said: *Food Before War . . . People of India Rise*. A million people would die of starvation in the next year—perhaps twice that many except for the U.S. wheat surplus that was being pumped into the country, Jason recalled. But with the highest birth-rate and one of the lowest crop yields in the world, three-quarters of the population was always hungry.

He prodded Mr. Chatterji through the mob, concealing the .38 with a soggy newspaper. His reservation had gotten lost, and the young Indian desk clerk broke into a profuse stream of apologies. Not too many westerners stayed at the Great Punjab any more . . . it was regrettable . . . such a fine hotel . . . the British had loved it . . . He punctuated his last sentence with a kick that sent his assistant scrambling toward the old-fashioned telephone.

"Never mind," said Jason. "Has a Mr. Adam Cyber checked in?"

He had, and a minute later Jason and his prisoner

were ascending to the fifth floor on a creaking elevator. The faded old hotel had been chosen with care—the perfect place to stay out of sight and, hopefully, out of trouble.

The green-eyed, smooth-skinned man who shared Jason's past, present and future was not inside the hideously decorated room. Jason's eyes swept across moldy carpet to the rotting curtains that were billowing in the breeze coming through the open doors to the veranda. Shoving Mr. Chatterji ahead of him, he stepped over the threshold leading to the balcony.

Cyber was there. He was too preoccupied to bother with Jason's greeting.

His naked body glistened under the softly falling rain. It was contorted into the most difficult of all the classic Yoga positions—the *Padmasana* or Lotus, with three contractions. His eyes were closed and there was no sign of respiration.

Jason tapped his friend's forehead gently. Then he nudged Mr. Chatterji back inside the room and they waited. Three minutes later, Cyber appeared.

"It is a worthwhile discipline," he said. "A most interesting country. And you, my friend, have been in difficulty . . . or so your appearance would indicate."

Jason was a mess. His suit was covered with mud and worse. His face was a mass of bruises, sustained during the near disaster aboard the jet. He was exhausted and hungry . . . and there was still Mr. Chatterji.

"Adam," he said. "Our friend here has something to tell us. Only he can't quite bring himself to do it. Perhaps you can help him with his problem."

"What is it he would tell us?"

"The names of his friends—the ones who tried to murder me three times in the last forty-eight hours," said Jason, looking at Mr. Chatterji, whose brown face was in the process of losing all of its color.

"I see." Adam stood still for a minute. Then he started toward the sullen-faced Indian.

"Death will come before I reveal anything," Mr. Chatterji snarled. His eyes grew wider, and he trembled.

Then, strangely, his body relaxed. Adam's hand had brushed his pallid forehead. Mr. Chatterji's head slumped down until his chin was hanging on his chest, and his eyes slid shut. It wasn't hypnotism, thought Jason. It was more like something or someone had entered his body to take control of it, to tell it things that it had no power to resist.

Now Mr. Chatterji sat up again. His eyes opened and he stared blankly ahead. Adam's hand remained on his forehead.

"He is prepared for the questioning," said Adam.

"You were given instructions to destroy me. Why?" said Jason.

Mr. Chatterji's voice was hollow and far-away. "The Brotherhood does not question its commands. You are to be silenced. That is our task," he said.

"What is the Brotherhood?"

"Only the Leader knows."

"Where is the Leader?" asked Jason. Of course, the Indian was only a stooge, a hatchet man for an organization that called itself the Brotherhood.

"The Leader is everywhere. The Leader rewards and the Leader destroys," the Indian chanted it like an often-sung hymn.

"How does the Leader reward you?"

"With pleasures undreamed of."

"What else does he do?"

"The Leader heals the sick, repairs the wounded, comforts the dying." The little Indian's face lit up with the expectant look of a child about to be fed a lollipop.

"Does the Brotherhood know we are here?" Jason said, suspecting the answer before it came.

"The Brotherhood is watching you now," was the reply.

"Then they know that you are my prisoner," said Jason. "What will they do to you?"

"Death to all who reveal the secrets of the Leader," the little man said in a sad voice.

Jason found himself feeling a little sorry for the Indian. If the strange organization calling itself the Brotherhood was really as omnipotent as it claimed, the little fellow's life wasn't worth an inflated Indian rupee. Then he remembered the howling mob that had tried to tear him to pieces. Whatever happens to Mr. Chatterji is well deserved, he thought.

"That's all for now, Adam," he told his friend.

Adam's hand left the Indian's forehead and, a few seconds later, Mr. Chatterji's eyes blinked back into focus.

"I refuse to tell you anything, you heathen swine," he hissed.

"Quite right," said Jason. "Sorry we tried to make you." Then, turning to Adam, he suggested that Mr. Chatterji be temporarily put away for safekeeping. A heavy piece of window sash served for binding and the musty smelling closet for a storage place. When the door was shut, Jason went to the old telephone and, after a few calculated smashes across its rusty face, got through to the switchboard.

"Get me the Oceanic Trading Company," he said, reading the number off the piece of paper that Hamilton had scrawled on. "Mr. Joseph Blake," it said. "Trade Representative for India." The CIA could use a good idea man, thought Jason. By now everybody knows the import-export front as well as the face of a dollar bill.

Then the phone rang. Five and a half rings later, it was picked up and a pleasant male voice started to tell Jason that the Oceanic Trading Company was no longer in business, but any unpaid bills would be honored in due time.

"Look, Blake," he said. "This is Jason Starr, the guy your—ah—*company* told you to be looking for. . . ."

There was silence. Then the voice changed into its real self: "Yes, I received my instructions, what can I do for you, Mr. Starr?"

"We could have a little chat. Supposing I come around to your office," said Jason.

"About what, Mr. Starr?" The CIA man sounded suspicious. His orders were to keep out of Jason's affairs, and he wanted to keep his nose clean with Washington.

"Ever hear of an organization that calls itself the Brotherhood?" asked Jason softly. He heard the sharp intake of Blake's breath.

"I'll expect you in half an hour." The line went dead.

The streets were filled with jostling crowds carrying black umbrellas with bamboo handles, and everybody was trying to poke everybody's eyes out with their steel-ribbed edges. Hawkers screamed their wares from under rain-soaked archways; plastic pens, dime-store spectacles, combs, perfumed hair oil, elixirs to restore your sex life, elixirs to keep off the howling tribe of homeless beggar children who circled around you like a ragged swarm of flies. It was the oldest con game in the world, and Jason plunged through it, going toward the docks and his rendez-vous with Blake.

Cyber was on his way to the offices of the Bombay *Times* to search the newspaper's morgue for any leads that might show past activities of the Brotherhood, and Mr. Chatterji was resting peacefully in his closet, gagged with a clean silk handkerchief.

It was dark and still raining by the time Jason found the old warehouse with the faded sign—OCEANIC, LTD.—over its paintless single door. The door was slightly ajar, so he didn't bother to disturb the silence with a knock. He stepped inside and paused to let his eyes adjust to the darkness. He was standing in a large room filled with uneven stacks of cotton bales. A light burned dimly through a frosted glass door at the other end. The cotton smelled like it had been picked the year before Caesar was assassinated, and the rain drummed steadily on the tin roof. Jason started toward the door. An office, probably. Blake would be waiting for him.

Blake had grown tired of waiting. His head was on the old roll-top desk, and his sagging shoulders indicated a stupefying need for sleep. Blake had also forgotten to close up his filing cabinets, his safe and all the rest of the open cabinets and drawers in the room. The ripped-open manila folders stamped with big red letters that said TOP SECRET spilled out in all directions. Jason's eyes took it all in in a split second. He crossed over to the desk.

Even if he hadn't been dead, Blake wouldn't have done much talking.

His tongue had been cut out. He had choked to death on his own blood.

Just as Jason decided he was going to get sick, he noticed the blood-smeared marks on the back of a bill of lading underneath Blake's clenched right hand. His curiosity won the battle with his stomach, and he extracted the paper carefully.

It held the tongueless man's last three words. Written in his own blood, it said: *Krupt. ND. Kumindani.* A dried red fingerprint ended the message.

It had been a fast job. But thorough. Jason found nothing of importance in the open files or the safe. Krupt? Krupt? . . . the K section contained nothing but a list of known killers wanted by the Indian Bureau of Investigation.

Then, hidden in Blake's wallet in a false pocket they had apparently overlooked, he found Kumindani.

She was as beautiful in her way as Maria d'Allesandro Corday, the girl that Jason had left in Washington. She was wearing the ceremonial dress of an Indian classical dancer and her luminous dark eyes, her full-molded high breasts and her perfect legs said a lot for the Indians as a race. On the back of the picture she had written: *For Joey and joy . . . Kumindani.* Well, the joy part was over, thought Jason. He was halfway to the door before he remembered. The Brotherhood had murdered Blake *after* the telephone call. Meaning they knew he was here. Meaning he was due to be next on their agenda—even more so than before, probably. How? A bomb? Gas? Bullets? No. Another typically staged "accident." He remembered the dried-out old cotton in the main warehouse. Probably burns like an old widow's wig, he thought. They would be waiting now. He thought swiftly and his eyes searched the room quickly— wildly. Finally they found what they sought. Thank God the Indian power industry is so inefficient, he thought. A can of kerosene and a lantern were sitting in the corner next to the telephone.

Jason worked swiftly.

Using the CIA files, he built a paper snowball two feet high. He tied it together with a ball of twine from the top of the desk. Then he soaked it down with kerosene. He poured on some more while he was dialing the number of the Bombay *Times*. Hoping that the message reached Cyber, he told the newspaper morgue attendant to have his friend meet him at the airport.

He poured 'the rest of the kerosene into his snowball while he called the police.

"I say, old boy," he said to the duty sergeant. "Thought you ought to know—one hell of a blaze is raging down here at the Oceanic Trading Company . . . just doing my duty as a loyal ex-colonial official."

He hung up with the rapid "What . . . what . . . what" of the duty sergeant still buzzing in his ear.

Now let's see how my little assassins like their whiskers singed, he thought. Cutting an extra piece of twine, he carried his snowball to the door. While he tied down one end to the bomb and looped the other through his hand, he listened. Sooner or later someone has to cough, he thought.

He was right. It was actually a nervous throat being cleared somewhere in the darkness of the big outer loft. The Brotherhood *was* waiting.

Jason's cigarette lighter did nicely.

The snowball turned itself into a bomb of pure fire in five seconds. Jason waited until he could feel his fingertips starting to burn. Then his foot lashed out, shattering the glass door into a million fragments. He whirled his missile once around his head and let it fly.

It arched high, trailing fire like a comet, and then down, to explode in a shower of flaming debris on the wood floor. It scattered itself all over the high-stacked, tinder-dry bales of cotton, turning them into walls of flame. The quickness with which it all happened surprised even Jason. The stuff was going up as if it was impregnated with oil.

He dove through the small window at the back of the office head-first. It was the first time he was glad of the rain and the mud. He hit shoulder-first and rolled with the shock. By the time he had wiped off his eyes he was up and the .38 in his hand.

It was another alley, dark and empty—this was a dockside area—and he crossed over and took up a station behind a pile of broken masonry. The warehouse was uncannily silent. Some of them must be making it out through the front door, thought Jason. But not very many. Then he saw the head and shoulders appear in the window from which he had recently ejected himself. The silhouette of a man framed in fire. It started to climb out. Then Jason squeezed the trigger and it stopped. It fell back inside and disappeared.

There were two more. Jason was merciful. He hit them before they wasted any energy climbing out. The last one screamed before his arms slid out of sight. It was silent for a moment. Then the whole world exploded. Jason had a flash view of the top of the warehouse rising into the night sky on a pillar of fire, and the shock wave drove his face back into the mud.

He let it stay there for a while. In fact, he was most grateful to it. While secondary explosions rocked him back and forth, and wreckage pelted across the top of the pile of broken masonry, he hugged the ooze, thinking. Rotten old cotton bales, full of high explosives—the CIA warehouse, all right, and also the CIA's depot for demolition materials. I guess some explanations will be in order if and when I have a chance to make them, he thought. A last minor explosion rocked the building.

The wail of sirens interrupted his reveries. It was the police and the fire department. Time for Jason to disappear—unless he wanted to do his explaining from an Indian jail cell. As he trotted away through the darkness, he heard the distant popgun sounds of small-arms fire. Apparently the police were cleaning up the surviving members of the Brotherhood's strong-arm squad. He slowed to a walk, and while he made his way through the oldest slum in ancient Bombay, his mind started to glue the bits and pieces of new information together.

Strangely enough they stuck: Mr. Chatterji, the so-called Brotherhood, Kumindani . . . Krupt . . . and ND. New Delhi, of course! The site of the symposium of brain researchers and cybernetic specialists . . . the arrows all pointed in that direction. And tomorrow was the day the conference began. Satisfied with his decision, Jason stopped thinking and trotted toward the lights of the main thoroughfare that lay a block ahead. The rain was slackening off and a shaft of cold moonlight found its way through the clouds long enough to illuminate his strong, high-cheek-boned face. It was the face of a man who was learning the laws of the jungle and the art of survival.

Chapter †
ELEVEN

THE INDIAN PEOPLE are said to be the world's largest and most disorderly welcoming committee. This fact and this fact alone was responsible for saving Jason's rumpled tropical suit from the effects of the five well-positioned and accurately aimed high-velocity hunting rifles aimed at his chest by five well-hidden men.

The crowd, which numbered in the hundreds of thousands, had been waiting under the hot Punjab sun for more than three hours. They had been waiting for the leading Chinese delegate to the Asian symposium on Human Development—Doctor Hsin Lau, a man of peace and a man of hope. Science knows no political boundaries, and the current border crisis with China had not prevented the Indian Congress Party from turning its members out en masse to welcome the good doctor and the other delegates. It was good official policy and great fun.

As the Air India DC-3 with Jason and Adam aboard cut its engines and creaked to a stop in front of the New Delhi Air Terminal, a tiny speck appeared in the blue sky. By the time the door of the thirty-year-old aircraft had been flung open, the speck had grown into an Illyushin jetliner with two large red stars painted across its fuselage. It was the Chinese delegation, and the crowd knew it.

As Jason ducked through the door into the swelter-ing mid-morning heat followed by Cyber, a great roar went up from thousands of Hindus.

What happened next saved Jason's life.

With one accord, the people surged forward. The steel retaining fences toppled. The line of policemen was swept aside, and the howling mob surged onto the field.

An instant later Jason felt rather than heard the sighing swish of a high-powered bullet going past his head. A hole appeared in the aluminum over the door. Then another. Then the man ahead of Jason, a minor Indian bureaucrat with whom he had exchanged a few words on the flight, jerked spasmodically and pitched forward down the ramp.

"The crowd! Quickly!" Jason's words were swal-lowed up in the general pandemonium. With Adam right behind him, he hurdled the body of the Indian and they were swept into the center of the welcom-ing mob.

Women screamed. Children tried to escape and were caught in a forest of grown-up legs. Everywhere, policemen swung their bamboo *lathis*, smashing them down on heads that paid no heed. Somewhere a pipe-band was playing what once might have been the Indian national anthem. But still the human tidal wave pressed forward. Its goal was the awning-cov-ered platform which was to be used to receive the dignitaries.

The mob overran it just as the big jet rolled to a stop, and the startled Chinese pilot cut his engines hurriedly for fear of sucking a few score heads into them. The line of top-hatted officials was swallowed up in a flash. Chairs, tables, microphones were over-turned and trampled to kindling. The awning sagged badly and then slid off its supports, covering the rest of the scene like a modest veil. Underneath it the game went on until, one by one, shirtless, hatless and shoeless government officials emerged. The police rushed forward and the battle continued.

Somehow Jason and Cyber had managed to hang back during the melee. Now they found themselves on the edge of the vast crowd centered around the parked jetliner. As the ramp dropped and the first Chinese emerged, Jason saw the way out of their desperate situation.

It was an old Packard limousine, parked in a line of newer cars with flags attached to the fenders . . . part of the motorcade into town. The autos stood deserted, and Jason beckoned his friend forward. The Chinese were emerging now, and the crowd roared its approval. Since the reviewing stand lay in wreckage, the visiting dignitaries were surrounded by a cordon of police and led swiftly to the cars which would deliver them to Government Palace and a garden party.

The ten-mile drive into New Delhi was a continuation of the Indian madness for good will. Flags had been planted, flower covered archways erected, and the motorcade roared past a colorful cheering rose-pelting throng. Jason was in ninth place. He drove with one hand and brushed the flower petals out of his eyes with the other. Beside him Cyber turned his head left and right. He seemed interested in the spectacle.

"Smile, Adam," said Jason. "Wave your arm . . . it's part of being in a parade." It's also part of giving the Brotherhood the slip, at least for the time being, he thought.

Sitting up to their waists in crushed flowers, they drove past saluting sentries and parked in the Palace courtyard. They got out and followed the crowd streaming through a stone gateway and up a staircase leading to the gardens of *Rashtrapati Bhavan*.

What looked like three thousand people eddied and swirled along the paths between the flowerbeds and fountains. Above Jason, the old viceroy's palace looked down. A magnificently uniformed band played military airs, and turban-clad sikhs hovered behind long tables waiting to serve tea. Jason could have eaten a sacred cow at that point, but tea it was, and tea he would drink.

The Chinese had disappeared inside the Palace and now, with a fanfare of trumpets and the first bar of the national anthem, they reappeared, coming down one of the pathways toward Jason. He recognized Dr. Lau immediately. Tall for a Chinese, with a full head of graying hair. The eyes were practically lidless, and cold. Very cold. Walking beside him was a Westerner, a huge man with a coarse, piglike face and a close-cropped bristle of rust-red hair. Ignoring the happy greetings that peppered them from all directions, the two men moved stolidly through the greeters, engaged in conversation. Jason saw the redhead nod rapidly as if he had agreed to something and then turn away from the doctor to disappear into the crowd. Then the party passed on and Jason's eyes fell on the tea tables. There were cakes and cookies, too.

"Come on," he said to Cyber. "I could eat a ton of those." Cyber seemed as famished as Jason. Usually, the man from the future seemed to eat very little or not at all. It was as if eating was an experiment for him, a sampling of an antique custom.

But Jason was outflanked before he could reach the free food. A motley crowd of guests descended on the service and staged an elbow-swinging, cup-balancing free-for-all. Jason watched it and groaned.

Then the blare of trumpets from the corner of the

garden announced the afternoon's entertainment. A small stage had been put up and, as Jason and Cyber made their way toward it, the sound of cymbals, the tinkle of strings and the throb of a drum came forth. The crowd hushed and a voice announced in English: "Good afternoon ladies and gentlemen—for your diversion, we present the classical dances of India."

She danced the sacred dance of *Shiva,* who is the creator, the destroyer, who haunts graveyards and is the lord of ghosts. She played the part of one of *Shiva's* many wives, *Kali*—who likes human sacrifices. With the consummate grace of a great dancer, she moved her exquisitely formed body in the ritual motions of lust. Then, as *Sati,* she sacrificed herself to her lord by leaping into the imaginary flames, the ritual act of *suttee,* the centuries-old curse of Hindu widows. As she danced, Jason watched the delicate face. It never changed expression, and when she bowed low at the end of her performance, Kumindani's eyes flickered once in the direction of the Chinese delegation, where Dr. Hsin Lau sat, his face frozen into an impenetrable mask. Kumindani's eyes were full of hate.

After the dance Jason left Cyber to keep an eye on the doctor and worked his way through the departing audience around to the back of the stage. The musicians were packing up their instruments. There was no sign of the girl whose picture he had found in the dead CIA man's wallet. Kumindani had disappeared.

Then he saw a *sari*-clad figure walking swiftly down the path leading to the palace. The lovely and sensual movement of her hips was unmistakable. He caught up with her just before she turned a corner full of old statuary. His fingers sank into a lusciously curved shoulder, his nose filled with the most exotic perfume it had ever smelled, and he said, "Kumindani, I need your help."

"Who are you?" cried the girl as she spun around, and Jason found himself looking into a pair of startled deep brown eyes. Then his glance fell to the full red lips and the startlingly white teeth. She was the most beautiful Indian girl he had ever seen.

"Jason Starr," he said. "A friend of Joe Blake."

"Joey!" The brown eyes looked frightened. "What do you want? What have they done to him?"

"It's a long story, and we both might be dead before I get the chance to finish it," said Jason. He pulled out Blake's picture and gave it to the girl. He could tell that she understood. Her face lost color, and a sudden shudder ran through her delicate body.

"I've got to talk to you," he said.

"Very well, Mr. Starr. But not here. Follow me." She led him swiftly through the remainder of the garden, and they slipped out a side entrance into the crowded streets of New Delhi. In a few minutes Jason was lost. He thought of Cyber. How to find him wouldn't be a problem. They had agreed to meet at sundown in front of the parliament building, a landmark both of them could locate easily.

Kumindani led him through the usual maze of unplanned dwellings. Finally, she halted and motioned him through a heavy wooden door set in a high wall. They had entered a large courtyard, the private garden of some wealthy Hindu, Jason guessed. Huge banyan trees thrust upward, cutting off the mid-day sun.

"My family's summer villa," the girl explained. "We are safe here." She sank down on a stone bench underneath one of the trees, and Jason followed suit.

"How did he die, Mr. Starr?" Kumindani asked.

"Call me Jason," he said gently. "It isn't the kind of death I care to describe in detail, expecially to the woman who loved him."

"Yes, I loved him," Kumindani's eyes were hard. "In spite of his work."

"We can't all choose our jobs," said Jason. "You dance, Blake worked for the CIA, and I get chased all over the world by a happy little group of murderers that calls itself the Brotherhood."

"The Brotherhood!" There was a sharp intake of breath. For the first time the girl's eyes showed fear. It was only there for an instant before she got it back under control—but it was there. "What do you know about the Brotherhood?" she whispered.

"What do you know about a man named Krupt?"

She paused to let the name sink in. Then she said, "Otto Krupt is the wealthiest man in New Delhi. He's a physician. He specializes in restoring the jaded appetites of a certain segment of our Indian leadership. The sexual appetites."

"What else?"

"Krupt is an ex-Nazi. It's common knowledge he was in charge of 'human experimentation' at one of the death camps in Poland. But his influence in high government circles is strong enough to force even the honest to leave him alone. As the saying goes, Mr. Jason Starr, 'In India the strength in a man's loins is more important than the strength of his character.'"

"Do you know Krupt personally?" So far Jason was impressed with the girl's answers. The next one was even more honest.

"Otto Krupt raped me five years ago," she said as if it had been a totally unimportant incident in her life. "I was nineteen years old, just back from the University of London. I met him at a diplomatic reception. He asked me to dance at one of his private

102

parties. He seemed civilized enough . . . in spite of his physical ugliness. I accepted. The party turned into a filthy orgy . . . the Marquis de Sade would have enjoyed himself. Krupt employs a group of Chinese—I think they're eunuchs. Krupt forced his tongue into my mouth in what he thought was a passionate kiss, and when I bit it almost in half he had them carry me upstairs and hold me down while he had his way with me." She finished, her eyes on Jason.

"And then what?"

"Some time later I met Joe Blake. I never told him what had happened. When he asked me to report anything I could find out about Krupt's activities, by then it was too late. Joe was in love with me. He would have tried to kill him, and I wanted Joe alive more than I wanted Otto Krupt dead."

"Were you in love with Blake?"

"Love, Mr. Starr?" The girl smiled, and suddenly she looked old, very old. "I am an agent of the Indian government and, like yourself, I have been taught to ignore the emotion. Unfortunately, Joe Blake had not. I let him 'love' me. It was convenient. It established trust between us. I'm sorry he's dead—is that enough?" she said, her eyes on him.

The girl thought he was a CIA man, and Jason decided to let her continue believing it.

"Krupt's activities—did you uncover anything?"

"Yes. I told Krupt I'd forget the whole episode on the condition that he behaved himself in the future. Even though the man's a beast, he has a German's sense of honor. He agreed. He's never touched me again. I dance at his parties. I leave early in the evening—before the real fun starts." Kumindani shivered. "I keep my eyes open and listen. Joe needed all the help he could get."

"Did Krupt ever mention the Brotherhood?"

"No, not directly. But, at every party he has a different group of people. Important-looking people. Big business and—what do you call it in America—the crime people . . . the Mafia."

"One more question," said Jason. "What does he look like?"

"He looks like a wild boar—a red-haired wild boar," said Kumindani.

The man walking beside Dr. Hsin Lau at the garden party, the man with the pink eyes and the red bristles. Jason's mind started working at high speed. Things were starting to fall into place.

"Do you know anything about Doctor Hsin Lau?" he asked the girl.

"Very little. Except that he is staying at Otto's villa during the symposium." The girl's forehead wrinkled up in an effort to remember. ". . . dance there tonight. And yes, the doctor has announced that he is too busy on some project or other to accept any social engagements. In fact, it is reported that a daily courier plane will leave New Delhi for China with Dr. Lau's dispatches aboard."

Yes, thought Jason. The CIA computer hit the nail all the way through the wall. The doctor was using his spare time to keep his staff working around the clock on the control equipment—his, Jason's, control equipment. Meanwhile, Lau was keeping up appearances . . . playing it safe until the thought-control machine could be put to work.

"Kumindani, you can pull out of this right now." Jason looked at the soft-skinned, delicate-featured girl. His eyes couldn't help noticing how high the *sari* was riding up her voluptuous brown inner thigh. "In fact, there's nothing more for you to prove. So thanks for the help." Jason stood up. "Forget you ever saw me, and in the future, stay away from Otto Krupt."

Before Jason could turn himself around and march himself away like the boy scout he was trying to be, two warm soft feminine arms reached out, circled his waist, and pulled.

"Mr. Jason Starr, you are—how do they say it—a ham when it comes to playing the role," two warm lips whispered in his ear. Then the lips made a trail around to the front of his face and found a second pair waiting for them. It was a long, excitingly sweet exchange of suggestive ideas.

"We must help each other," the girl said, kissing his neck. "What you do for yourself, I do for the memory of Joe Blake."

In a way Jason was glad that Blake was only a memory.

The Indian girl took his hand and led him inside the cool old house. She disappeared into a marble-floored bathroom. Jason heard water running, the sound of zippers unzipping, then silence. I didn't know *saris* had zippers, he reflected. Then the girl called to him.

She was splashing around a sunken tub at least as big as the one Liz Taylor had used in *Cleopatra*. And this one wasn't cluttered up with cameramen and assistant directors. Kumindani floated in the milky-warm water, her breasts bobbing on the surface like ripe peaches. Her eyes said it and Jason did it.

He slipped out of his clothes and joined her in the bath.

As he stepped down into the promising steamy depths, her slippery arms stretched out to encircle his broad shoulders. They slid together and Kumindani gave a throaty expectant chuckle. Jason studied her limpid black eyes through the rising vapor and was aware of her hands discovering his submerged body.

He pulled her head back, smoothing the long dark

105

hair into the water. Then he kissed her sinuous neck and explored her mouth, feeling her body draw taut to his touch. She clung to him and their arms and legs slowly intertwined.

"Now, American!" she cried expectantly. "Now!"

Later, after their love-making had continued on drier ground until both of them lay exhausted, Jason told her the parts of the story that she had to know in order to help him. Then he had more questions.

"Dr. Lau's laboratories—location and defenses—it's a tricky business—whatever you do, don't let them think you're overly interested," he said.

"Don't worry, my lover, there are ways," Kumindani's long, smooth thigh pressed against his own. She was a curious girl, thought Jason. A combination of English and Indian culture, lost unless she could have both.

"Krupt's bungalow, what's the layout? Does he do all of his work there?" he asked.

"I have heard that many strange men come and go in the night. Some have entered never to return, but nothing can be proven. It was once a Mogul king's palace. There are many rooms where the guests are not allowed. The grounds are guarded by men with rifles day and night." The girl trembled and pressed herself against Jason's chest. "Be careful, you are already precious to me," she whispered.

There was no time for care, Jason thought. Not with each second bringing the world closer to the end of civilization. He rolled over and sat up. It was time to find his Mind Brother and begin planning the night's activities.

He arranged a meeting place with the girl for the following day and started to climb into his soiled clothes. Kumindani stopped him.

"Those who wish to remain themselves in India dress according to the blindness of others," the girl said. Jason remembered his *Kim*, the story of the beggar boy who was a master of the quick change in costume and personality. He let her soft hands dress him in native garb without complaint. Then he kissed her and slipped out through the old garden 'nto the late afternoon sun.

It WAS ALMOST absurdly easy. Or perhaps breaking into CIA headquarters was ten times as hard, thought Jason.

A yellow Punjabi moon hung low on the horizon, lighting their way through the tumble-down grounds that surrounded the huge high walled old Mogul palace with its red sandstone parapets gleaming like a hundred sullen eyes in the night. They avoided the armed guards easily and, with Cyber leading, they flitted from tree to tree, using ruined *ghats* and deserted outbuildings for cover. They entered the palace through a deserted courtyard full of rusting garden furniture. The Mogul emperors had lasted for more than four centuries; in its death rattle, the seedy system had turned its remaining energies from war to pleasure—a typically Indian response.

Inside the palace they made their way silently through vast rooms, up great staircases and along endless corridors, in and out of banquet halls, antechambers, throne rooms and hidden gardens. The moldering smell of decay was everywhere. At last they heard sound. It was music—cymbals, drums and flutes—and wild laughter rose over its steady rhythms. They rounded a corner, and Jason gasped at the scene that lay below.

From an inner parapet they were staring down at a huge garden. Jason guessed that it was at the center of the whole palace. The place was festooned with gaily colored lanterns which threw a shivering veil of light over the celebrants. And the celebration was in full swing. A hundred people were scattered around a central platform, lying on low divans and indulging themselves from the groaning tables filled with food and aphrodisiacs placed in front of them. Most of them were ignoring the half-naked girls who were everywhere, serving wine and food and making no attempt to avoid the lascivious hands that explored their bodies as they passed among the guests. Most of the guests were concentrating on the small stage. The reason was obvious. A man and a woman had just come out from a hidden doorway that led up from underneath. Both of them were naked.

What followed was too awful for Jason to watch. Dancing slowly to the pulsing beat of Indian drums, the naked couple approached each other. In slow motion, they assumed a variety of separate erotic postures designed to stimulate the audience. The teaser had its effect and the watching crowd applauded and called for more. The drum beat picked up, and then Jason stopped watching. The last thing he saw before he and Cyber slipped away was the couple's single fused and writhing shadow cast on the wall of the courtyard by the flickering light. As he and Cyber slipped back into the shadows seeking a way down, he heard more laughter and then thunderous applause. This was what Kumindani had mentioned when she had explained her early departures from Krupt's so-called "entertainments." And it was just beginning, he suspected.

There had been no sign of the red-haired German or of Dr. Hsin Lau. Perhaps they were too preoccupied with Lau's urgent work to indulge themselves—for this evening, anyway.

A series of open doors led them downward until Jason judged they were below the main floors of the palace. The passageway continued to slope and the air grew steadily cooler. From somewhere Jason heard the sound of dripping water.

The tunnel leveled out. They seemed to have entered a larger chamber. Jason felt through the folds of his *dhoti* until he found his lighter. He flicked it and, in the sudden glow, saw that they were standing in a high-ceilinged triangular chamber. At the apex of the triangle, a heavy steel bank-vault door blocked further progress. It was Krupt's secret storehouse. A real stroke of luck, thought Jason. Behind that door were the answers he needed. All he had to do was to get it open.

"Adam, have you ever heard of a combination lock?" he said to his silent companion. He explained the principles of the device, and Cyber nodded.

"It is a simple mechanical problem," his low voice rumbled in the darkness. Jason followed his footsteps toward the safe door. He heard the dial spin and the click of tumblers. Then silence. Then one more spin and a final click.

"The device is even simpler than I thought," said Cyber. "It is cleared. The door will open."

- Together they swung the heavy door open and entered. A musty smell rose up around them. Also another smell—a fetid odor—almost like wild animals, thought Jason. He flicked his lighter on again.

Then it happened. Actually two things. The heavy safe door rumbled shut on its rusted hinges, and a set of steel bars dropped in front of it from a hidden recess in the ceiling. It had been too simple, Jason realized. Too simple to enter the palace, too simple to find their way through the maze of corridors and to open doors, and too simple to open the safe. They had been led by the nose without a squeak, and now it was too late. They would suffer the consequences. Kumindani, he thought. What a fool I was! The girl had told Krupt. She was no Indian agent. Probably the German's mistress all along. That would explain Blake's death at the hands of the Brotherhood.

The consequences of his mistake were not long in coming.

Jason flashed his lighter around the vault. It was a strange-looking vault. The floor was covered with sand instead of concrete. There were no signs that it had been used for storage; and, at the far end, there was a low steel access door. As Jason approached it, it started to slide upward into the rock. As it did so, a strong pungent odor made him retreat.

It was an odor he knew. It was the smell of cats. Big cats. The kind the Indians called man-eaters. Then he saw it—the yellow eyes of Satan gleaming in the lighter's flame, the orange and white ruff standing up to signal the kill. It was a huge Bengal tiger. With a roar of hunger it came hurtling out of the passage, all 1,500 pounds of it. Jason never finished his spring to one side. He felt a furry avalanche descend on him, and then he was flying through the darkness toward something bright which exploded inside his head.

It was still pitch-black when he came to. He was lying on the sand, and his chest felt like it had been operated on with a baseball bat. Groaning, he sat up. Then he heard something in the darkness, something very familiar.

It was a throaty purr.

Somehow he found the lighter. The scene that met his eyes was ridiculous. It was also unbelievable. The big cat was lying on its side, its chest heaving in and out, its tail swishing and its head resting in Cyber's lap. Cyber was stroking it absent-mindedly as if it were an ordinary house kitten that had decided it needed a little attention. Jason felt like laughing. Instead he got up—slowly and carefully, just in case. But the big tiger ignored him. It was enjoying itself too much.

"How in hell's name did you do *that*?" asked Jason.

"The animal has been mistreated," said Cyber, tickling his ears. "Left without food, beaten and intimidated to do violence by its human masters. I—communicated—with it. It will obey."

That still didn't explain *how* Cyber had "communicated" with it, but Jason decided to wait for further explanations. It was time to figure a way out of Otto Krupt's trap.

The little door through which the beast had entered to devour them was still open. Apparently Krupt or his men had assured themselves that the feast was under way and then had left. Probably to sample the fruits of the orgy still taking place, Jason thought.

The passage was long and low. It ended inside a cage that occupied one corner of a large room. There were other cages. The occupants snarled a vicious greeting. One whole wall was barred across, and Jason could see why. A huge bull elephant paced nervously back and forth inside, its trunk as thick as a man's body, its eyes red-rimmed with hate and misery. There was a simple gate barring the tiger's lair, and Jason raised it and stepped down. Cyber and the tranquilized beast followed.

He approached the elephant's prison and was rewarded with a baleful glare and a dangerous swipe from the creature's hairy trunk. Whoever had tortured the tiger had done an even better job on the elephant. Deep red welts ran down its sides, and its tender and sensitive ears had been run through with sharp-pointed instruments. It was further evidence of the kind of cruelty that is practiced by a totally perverted mind. Jason felt the anger rising up within him. He let it. It would be useful for what he planned to do next.

"Adam," he said, "you seem to have quite a way with angry animals. See what you can do about calming our disturbed friend down, will you?"

Whatever Adam did, it worked. In a few minutes the elephant was practically crooning to itself and its trunk was waving good-naturedly through the bars at both Adam and Jason. When they opened the door, it came out as quietly as a lamb and stood, hulking over them, a four-ton bundle of friendliness and good will.

"Let's get started," said Adam. "I have a feeling that our friends are about to stop enjoying the evening."

Jason was wrong for the second time in two hours. The night's entertainment was just getting started for Otto Krupt. It was a private entertainment and it was taking place in a different part of the ancient building. A part that Jason, Adam and their two animal companions located by the screams issuing from the balcony-circled room where twenty-five members of the inner council of the Brotherhood were seated in old-fashioned leather chairs, facing a dais with a lectern, a surgeon's table, and an ordinary wicker basket. By the time Jason and his companions had arrived the screaming stopped.

Both the patient and the lecturing doctor were already familiar to Jason. From his vantage point behind the curtained balcony, he was looking at the top of the close-cropped red hair of Otto Krupt's head. He was also looking into the luminously terrified eyes of Mr. Chatterji, who was belted firmly to the surgeon's table with heavy leather straps.

Krupt even had a form of pointer. It was a swagger stick. He rapped it twice across the lectern, and the room grew silent.

"Members of the Brotherhood," he began, "you have just witnessed the treatment we reserve for our enemies. Now you will see a further demonstration—a demonstration that the good Dr. Lau, our Chinese ally, has suggested as most fitting in dealing with informers," he said. Krupt's swagger stick tapped Mr. Chatterji across the forehead lightly. Mr. Chatterji winced.

Jason thought swiftly. So the Brotherhood had overheard everything that the taxi-driver-hatchet-man had bleated out in the Bombay hotel room. Now he was paying the price. Then Jason's blood ran cold. Krupt had referred to his "enemies." This was the second of two demonstrations—the screams he had heard—suddenly he knew why they had been so high-pitched. Kumindani had been the first victim for the Nazi doctor's torture table. So she had not told the German anything, and she was now probably dead. Jason's hand found the .38. He had it lined up with fat folds on the back of the redhead's neck and his finger was moving back relentlessly on the trigger before he stopped. The girl was almost certainly dead. Somehow, she had given herself away and had paid the penalty. But he still needed the answers. He put the gun back into the *dhoti* and listened.

"Members, we have done well today," Krupt's cold, sneering voice swept through the room. "Following the instructions given me by the great leadership of

114

the Chinese People's Republic, I have succeeded in destroying the two Americans. Succeeded, I might add, where you had failed. At this moment their corpses are being digested by one of my hunting tigers." Krupt smiled malignantly.

"It was extremely important that these two be eliminated," he continued. "One of them, the man called Jason Starr, was responsible for the device that we are now perfecting. A device that will make the great people of China the benevolent masters of the world!" Krupt's voice echoed hollowly across the chamber. Mad, thought Jason. Mad like all the other mad dogs who played the roles of Third Reich supermen.

"And now—" Krupt's voice modulated into a deadly little whisper "—the demonstration." Krupt bent over and picked up the wicker basket. He was very careful with it, handling it like a basketful of eggs. He set it down for a second in order to reach inside the lectern and take out a pair of goggles. He put the goggles on and then he spoke:

"Gentlemen, inside this basket an extremely rare snake is waiting to strike its victim. The results should be both amusing and worthy of our scientific curiosity. The snake is fangless, a spitting cobra, found only in certain parts of Africa. It spits its venom in the victim's eye. The victim is completely safe so long as he makes no attempt to rub the irritant away. If he should do so, his itching will break the tiny capillaries that supply blood to his eyeball. Death follows swiftly, so I am told." Krupt moved behind the table and looked down at Mr. Chatterji. Suddenly his hand darted into the basket. It came up with the writhing, dun-colored body of an angry snake.

"You see that the victim's hands are secured," said

115

Krupt, holding the snake over his head. "This is simply to immobilize him during the snake's attack. Afterwards, we will release the victim's hands to see if his will power can sustain him against the quite severe irritation caused by the venom."

Jason had had enough. He watched the doctor wave the snake around in the air above Mr. Chatterji's head for a moment longer. Then he crawled back through the curtains and rejoined his friend. Thank god for high old hallways, he thought. The elephant was clearing the roof by several feet. The tiger paced nervously back and forth. Both animals were nervous, apparently smelling the snake.

It was now or never. In spite of Mr. Chatterji's guilt, Jason couldn't stand idly by and watch the man murdered.

"Tell your friends their keeper is waiting, Adam," Jason said, motioning forward.

As Mr. Chatterji's first scream bubbled up from the table below, Jason ripped down the heavy hangings that concealed his perch. He had just time enough to catch a glimpse of Krupt, holding the open-mouthed snake's head over Mr. Chatterji's face, when a blur of crimson swept by him, knocking him back against the stonework.

Snarling with rage, the tiger launched itself into space. It hit in the middle of the Brotherhood and went immediately to work. As the first unbelieving cries reached his ears, Jason felt something else. It was the elephant, coming through the low arch, dragging half of it with him onto the flimsy wooden balcony. The beast won the contest. The woodwork gave way and fell slowly to the floor below, cushioning its arrival with the smashed bodies of several members of the Brotherhood. Jason clung to the stone ledge that remained and watched the trumpeting cyclone of flesh go to work.

It was all over in a few minutes. Apparently, the Brotherhood had checked its weapons at the door. The tiger and the pachyderm stood, panting, in the middle of a bloody shambles. An occasional low groan could be heard from the pile of twisted, torn bodies. Hoping that Adam's control was still effective, Jason dropped to the floor. The tiger turned its blood-dripping jaws toward him, then looked away. The elephant ignored him entirely.

"The man with the red hair is not among the dead." It was Adam, who had followed him in his descent.

Jason walked toward the dais. Mr. Chatterji was still tied to his table. There was no sign of Krupt or the snake. The little Hindu's eyes were covered with yellowish fluid and he was still alive. Krupt had never had a chance to release his hands. The hands were drumming wildly and the body was jerking.

"Kill me, master, kill me before I go mad!" his voice implored.

"Listen to me," Jason whispered. "The girl, Kumindani. Where is she?"

"Please. Have mercy. Kill me!" the little Indian babbled.

"Not until you tell me about the girl," said Jason. He hated himself for withholding the raving man's final release, but it was necessary. His words cut through Mr. Chatterji's insanity long enough for him to give Jason the answer.

"The operating theater—behind the curtain," the Hindu croaked. "We were kept there . . ."

"Adam!" Jason whirled around. His friend was soothing the animals. "Come on, there isn't much

117

time." Krupt was away safely and probably alerting the rest of his forces. "Wait," he said, noticing the double doors at the far end of the room. "Let them out through there." With the animals loose, they might gain a few precious minutes on the Brother-hood.

When Adam had let his charges through the doors opening on the arched hall leading toward the main part of the palace, Jason had one last thing to do; he undid the heavy buckle on the strap binding Mr. Chatterji's right hand. Then he and Cyber slipped through the curtained doorway and ran down the silent passageway toward the operating theater.

Kumindani's eyes looked up at Jason. She tried to smile, but the smile changed into a long cough that brought arterial blood frothing up to her lips. The girl still lay on the wheeled cart that Krupt had used during his first demonstration. She was naked. Her body was covered with hundreds of pin-sized holes. An icepick-like blade lay beside her head. Krupt had lectured pleasantly, his blade rising and falling, never destroying a vital part completely, in a horrible dis-play of cool anatomical virtuosity, his voice soothing, demanding, demonstrating. A red hatred filled Ja-son's eyes. He snapped himself out of it. The girl was obviously dying. But she was still conscious.

"Kumindani, can you talk?" Jason's fingers stroked her blood-spattered hair. The girl nodded feebly, slightly.

"Dr. Lau . . . he pretended to desire me . . . it was his trick . . . he knew I was looking for informa-tion . . . he allowed me into his chambers . . . and —then—I found the papers . . . his work. He had intended to trap me. They took me here . . ." Kumindani's voice faded. She coughed more blood. Jason felt her pulse. It was almost gone.

"Adam, can you help her?" he asked quickly.

"She is past even my assistance," the man from the future said somberly. "If the repair facility were here, it could repair her." But Jason knew that the facility was now fifty thousand years away in the future.

"Did you find the location of his laboratories?" His question brought the half-conscious girl back from the shadows of death that were clouding her pale, still face.

"Yes . . . in *Bhotiyal* . . . Tibet as you call it . . . in the land of the high hills . . . near a lake known as Manasarovar. . . ." The girl's voice faltered. "Go to the monastery in Simla . . . there you will find a hill man to lead you . . . Da Tenzing, of the Sherpas. Go now before they . . ." Kumindani's eyes flickered rapidly. Her mouth opened as if she wanted to say something more. Then it stretched into the final taut grin of death.

Cyber's hand on his arm brought him back to his senses. He heard shouting and the sound of running feet. Then a gun was discharged somewhere in the distance. It was time to go. The girl was dead, another swift sacrifice in the game of life and death. Not in vain . . . I hope not in vain, Jason breathed, turning away.

The rampaging animals seemed to have created enough confusion to make their departure as easy as their entrance. The sounds of gunfire and screams faded as Jason and Adam worked their way through the deserted grounds until they again reached the network of twisting city streets.

Now what, thought Jason, looking at the pale, gleaming face of his companion? Both of them looked like half-crazy Hindus in their bloodstained *dhotis*, and Krupt would soon have his men scouring the city, bribing, threatening and demanding information from every frightened Indian who had seen them. Then Jason remembered what the girl Kumindani had said, ". . . in India those who wish to remain themselves dress according to the blindness of others." The tension passed out of Jason, and for the first time in many days he smiled.

"Adam, I think we have to hop a free train ride."

Chapter †
THIRTEEN

WITH THE HIGHEST RANGE of mountains in the world forming a dizzying ice-curtained backdrop, the wiry, sunburned Sherpa knelt on the rock-strewn brown earth and prostrated himself before the wayside shrine. The late afternoon sun cast superb patterns of red and gold across the incredible jagged fist of the mountain that rose up in front of him. It was *Nanda Devi*, the sacred mountain, and Da Tenzing, the leader of the Sherpas, was asking for its protection.

The small group of men waited until Da Tenzing had made his offerings to the gods. Heavily dressed in quilted jackets and fur hats and boots, they were Sherpas—men of the high mountains—and they knew that in days and nights ahead they would need divine protection.

Jason Starr followed the ceremonies with interest. Until the great expeditions to conquer Everest had been mounted, the Sherpas had been practically a lost tribe—living on the rugged border between Nepal and Tibet in isolated valleys and practicing a form of Buddhism and demon worship thousands of years old. The Himalayas are mystical, he thought, gazing up at the 25,000-foot finger of Nanda Devi. They were also a perfect place for the Chinese to hide a secret complex of laboratories.

It had taken them two weeks to climb up through the verdant lowlands into the high hills. Two weeks of the most arduous walking that Jason had ever experienced. The trail led through mist-covered gorges, along knife-edged ridges . . . up and down and up again . . . until his lungs burned fire and his legs turned to jelly. Now, after several days of it, he was keeping up with the squat little men who raced up narrow trails like mountain goats and who had offered him their lives with a savage abandon and a great laugh . . . as if it was a perfectly normal thing to do.

Da Tenzing rose. His eyes were snapping with merriment as he approached Jason.

"This night we will cross the border," he said. "The dogs of China will feel our bite."

Nanda Devi marked the division between Communist-controlled Tibet and Indian Kashmir. It was a border without agreement, a shifting no-man's land patrolled by both the Reds and the Indians, the site of so many "incidents" . . . incidents of sudden violence and mysterious silence. Through it lay Jason's and Adam's route to the shores of Lake Manasarovar.

Jason glanced at his friend, Adam, and chuckled. The man from the future looked more like a Sherpa, with his keen eyes and high-cheekboned features, than some of the Sherpas did themselves. He thought of the ride up from New Delhi to Simla. They had slipped aboard the slow-moving passenger train on the outskirts of the city. The ride had been an endless excursion across the hot plains, with Adam chattering endlessly in Hindi or whatever language he needed to use with their fellow sufferers in the third-class compartment. Jason remained silent, a dirty young northern Indian, who, Adam explained, was suffering from a mental disorder.

As Da Tenzing motioned the group forward again, Jason thought about his first meeting with the little Sherpa in the monastery at Simla. As soon as Jason had told him about Kumindani, Da Tenzing's face had twisted with rage and hatred. Apparently the Sherpa had worked with both Blake and the girl in their effort to uncover the activities of the Brotherhood. The mountain man grew very excited when Jason told him his plan to cross the border into Tibet. Before the Chinese had invaded and communized the "roof of the world," the Sherpas had played the role of middlemen in the thriving Tibetan-Indian trade routes. Now the border was closed and their Tibetan brothers were groaning under the yoke of Chinese rule. Da Tenzing had demanded that he and he alone lead the expedition. He was out for a double-edged vendetta. Jason thought of Otto Krupt—still free and probably murdering people by the score in his search for the two Americans. Someday, somehow he would find the German. He would give him a very fast death instead of the slow death which he deserved.

"We approach the frontier." Tenzing's voice floated back along the single column of men now moving behind the protective cover of a high, snow-covered ridge. He issued a staccato series of instructions, and the rest of the Sherpas deployed themselves behind rocks and boulders. Jason crept forward and had a look down over the cornice of ice and snow.

The Chinese were there, all right. A battalion of them camped against the base of the jagged precipice which he was peering over. They were settling down for the night, their fires of yak dung glowing cheerfully in the thin cold air. They were a pretty threadbare-looking bunch . . . strictly light infantry from the look of the two old, Russian-made trucks parked side-by-side in front of the largest tent. A line of World War II howitzers—the horse-drawn variety—was drawn up in a loose formation on the outskirts of the tent village. The People's Republic wasn't wasting time or money on its Indian border troops—not with Viet Nam at one end and Russia on the other to keep them occupied.

"What fools these slant-eyed sons of goats are," Da Tenzing now whispered into Jason's ear. "Only a headless chicken would build his nest under a wall of ice!"

The Sherpa moved off in the darkness, and Jason heard some stifled laughter. Whatever he had in mind, it wasn't going to improve the spirits of their Chinese brothers down below, thought Jason.

The muffled sounds of packs being opened made him withdraw from his vantage point. With Jason's money and Da Tenzing's experience as a guerilla fighter in Burma, the Sherpas had come well-supplied with the special weapons needed for their mission. Swiftly the men broke out packages of plastic explosives, detonating caps, and reels of wire. One by one they vanished into the shadows on top of the ice cornice. The sound of ice-axes picking into the frozen snow reached Jason's ears. Then the men returned trailing the wire.

"Down the slope! Quickly!" Tenzing urged.

Unreeling the wire behind them, they scrambled and slid until their feet touched firmer ground. Tenzing called a halt.

"An unfortunate accident." His white teeth flashed in the darkness. "Caused by the stupidity of their officers. In the spring the ice will melt. They will be found. Perhaps by the wolves before their thrice-cursed brothers."

Tenzing struck a match and, in the light cast by its glow, touched the two wires to the contact points on the detonator.

The result was terrifying and swift.

With an ear-shattering roar the charges erupted. The ground rose up and slugged Jason in the face. Through the buzzing in his ears he heard a slow and rising thunder. The whole opposite side of the cliff was giving way; a million tons of ice, snow and rock were hurtling onto the Chinese encampment. The thunder continued for many minutes. Then absolute silence. They started climbing back up the face at Tenzing's command.

Jason stared down at the patchwork quilt of snow and rock that half-filled the valley below, a white blanket of death covering a thousand Chinese soldiers . . . soldiers who had deserved, perhaps, a better fate than the one caused by their own carelessness. He turned away. It was time to go on.

The Sherpas led the way through a lunar-like landscape of boulders and outcroppings, the deposits left by retreating glaciers of a million years ago. Then, roped together, they crossed snow-fields whose glittering surfaces were crisscrossed by yawning crevasses. The bright full moon disappeared behind a range of distant peaks, leaving them in darkness. The sky began to show the beginnings of dawn. In spite of his conditioning, Jason constantly fought the desire to wearily fall in his tracks . . . to sleep, with every step. At last, as the first rays of the sun colored the peaks to the east, Da Tenzing called a halt.

"The valley of Lake Manasarovar lies below," the Sherpa said simply. "We will rest here."

As tired as he was, Jason waited for the sun to pierce the shadowy landscape that lay below. He had come halfway around the world, he had seen innocent people murdered and his career ruined . . . and now he would see the reason.

The sun rose over the mountain-ringed bowl, throwing its flat surface into harsh relief. The lake was large, and its fingers spread across the valley like spokes on a wheel. Its waters were flat and limitlessly blue in the morning calm. Nothing moved on its surface and nothing moved along its shore. It was a timeless, empty scene. It was a world that had existed forever, a world in which man had not intruded. The valley was empty!

The blood rose in his head, and he felt like smashing something with his bare fist. It was a great joke on them. A wild goosechase that made Wrong-Way Corrigan look right. A silly, stupid one-man operation that would keep them laughing for months inside the CIA's employees' lounges. He had started with no proof . . . he was finishing with no proof. It was hilarious. The Chinese had won the game.

A cool hand gripped his shoulder. "Listen," said Cyber, his green eyes full of some kind of special concentration.

Then Jason heard it.

It was the distant but unmistakable sound of an airplane, the steady throb of piston-driven engines. A speck appeared far to the East. It grew steadily larger until Jason's eyes could resolve a familiar shape. It was an old C-47, the military version of the DC-3, the two-engined workhorse of the last World War.

Now it was circling over Lake Manasarovar, spiraling down toward the flat desert floor, Red Chinese markings clearly visible on its brown wing-tips. The pilot lined up along an arm of the lake, dropped his flaps, and brought her in. Instead of fishtailing wildly

126

across the supposedly rugged surface of the make-shift landing place, the aircraft touched down smoothly and rolled straight. In a few seconds it was taxiing up to what looked, from Jason's vantage point, like a low hill with a few sparse bushes crowning its top. Then the pilot cut his engines and the plane rolled to a stop.

Then something strange happened.

The hill moved. It stretched like a thin sheet of gauze and came apart and, at the same time, Jason's eyes captured the true perspective of the scene which they had failed to perceive moments ago. He was looking at a well-camouflaged building. A low, concrete-walled structure covered with a skillfully designed net, supported by long bamboo poles. From two miles away it blended perfectly into the floor of the valley.

With his binoculars, Jason swept over the area. Other shapes resolved themselves—a whole complex of squat, one-story buildings floated through the shimmering heat. They were all camouflaged beautifully. The largest building was attached to an open, barbed-wire-enclosed compound with low towers on the perimeter. Tiny figures moved aimlessly across its bare surface. It looked like a prison camp. He swung back to the transport plane.

Its clamshell doors were opening, and the Chinese ground crew was swarming out of the building. A group of men started climbing down the short ladder from the plane, some of them in the drab military uniforms of the classless Chinese People's Army. Two of them were dressed in western clothes and, judging from the handshakes and bows, they seemed to be the big wheels. The whole group started toward the building. Then Jason's hand tightened around the binoculars—one of them had stopped. He turned around, and Jason caught the distant flash of carrot-red hair. Otto Krupt was paying a visit to his hard-working friend, Dr. Hsin Lau. The group moved away and Jason, his mind working rapidly, scrambled down behind the ledge where Da Tenzing and his men were snoring peacefully under the rays of the hot morning sun.

The Sherpa was awake and on his feet instantly. When Jason had described the situation, he moved up the ledge to have a look for himself. He came back down not looking as pleased as the night before.

"There are many Chinese, and they protect themselves with machine guns," he said quietly.

"Yes," agreed Jason, "except that the last thing they are expecting is what we're going to give them—a heavenly display of the wrath of the gods calculated to make their superstitious eyeballs pop out."

Chapter †
FOURTEEN

THE MOON HUNG on silver threads of wind-blown snow behind the twisted finger of Nanda Devi, its light varnishing the icy surface of the valley below. A keen, cold wind knifed down through the passes, raising swirls of dust up toward the black night sky, and lashed the surface of Lake Manasarovar into a white-toothed froth. Nothing moved except the wind. The sound of an occasional low moan came from the direction of the prison compound.

Crouched behind a cairn of granite, Jason shivered. He adjusted the fur flaps of his Sherpa hat and checked his watch for the hundredth time. Cyber lay beside him, a motionless dark figure whose eyes blazed green in the shadow. If everything went on schedule, in two minutes the makeshift device that he and Cyber had tinkered with all through the long afternoon would put itself into operation. On the other hand, it might fizzle . . . which would mean the end of the road for all of them.

The Sherpas were concentrated at the other end of the airstrip, ready to assault the machine gun emplacements that protected its open flank. Da Tenzing knew his business. The men were armed with lightweight mortars, grenades, burp guns, and what Tenzing called "the stinger," a forty-millimeter recoilless rifle, apparently smuggled into India and sold on the black market and secured as the spoils of some forgotten engagement in Viet Nam.

Jason had a few toys of his own: phosphorous grenades, a Thompson sub-machine gun, and a rucksack full of plastiques, each with a radio-controlled detonator. Cyber, as usual, went empty-handed. The man from the future had never, to Jason's knowledge, picked up a weapon, except to examine it as if it were some kind of medieval curiosity . . . worthy of children, perhaps, but useless to him.

On the other hand, without Cyber's help, Jason would never have completed his machinery, the machinery that was now resting three miles away on a high ledge under the peak of Nanda Devi. They had built it out of wood, tin cans, and electrical tape; it was the weirdest-looking contraption that man or gods had ever seen. A home-made rocket ten feet long and a foot in diameter . . . except where the skin bulged in the wrong places. It was sitting on a makeshift trough that angled toward an imaginary point a half-mile above the center of the lake. It was a two-stage affair, powered by a solid fuel of Cyber's concocting. It was a combination of gunpowder, high explosive, and pulverized rock. "Naturally occurring silicates and nitrates," Cyber had explained. The whole mess had been bound into two solid lumps with a rubber raincoat melted over a well-hidden slow fire. The payload? Well, that was something else again, and that something he would soon see.

Jason didn't have long to wait. Thirty seconds later, a shower of sparks appeared on the distant ridge. The home-made time fuse had ignited stage one on schedule. Trailing a plume of fire, his rocket mounted into the night sky. It pitched over into its pre-planned arc as the burning fuel changed its center of gravity—a primitive but effective guidance system, thought Jason. As the fiery trail reached its zenith, he began to count down the seconds on his wristwatch.

With a distant pop, the payload was ignited by the last of the burning propellant. A half-second later, Lake Manasarovar and the entire valley was ablaze with incredibly bright light. A huge, whirling ball of fire appeared in the sky over the lake. Great tentacles of red, orange and green flame shot out from the incandescent central core. It looked as if the sun had gone insane and was destroying itself.

Even Jason was impressed with his handiwork. The mixture of phosphorus and magnesium—stripped from twenty grenades—and the oil-soaked rags was providing part of the diversion they would need before the attack began. The other part was under his direction. As the fireball floated over the valley on its jury-rigged parachute, his hand poised over the radio-detonator. A few more seconds passed as the fireball consumed itself. Then, as the intense heat melted through the dynamite-filled metal core of the device, it exploded into a million glowing fragments, which quickly winked out, plunging the valley into darkness.

Jason pressed the little button on the small box, setting off the charges placed across the great snow cliffs that brooded over the arid valley. A roar went up. It was soon replaced by a growing thunder as the walls gave way and avalanched down toward the opposite shore of the lake.

"Let's go, Adam," Jason whispered, scrambling over the rocks that had served them as a hiding place. The display was over. If it had worked, the complex should be in an uproar. The half-educated Chinese soldiers were a superstitious lot. When the heavens blew up in their faces, there was no telling what their first reaction would be.

Jason wasn't long in finding out.

He and Adam ran toward the main building, now a plainly visible silhouette under its truncated camouflage net. As they approached, Jason heard a strange sound. It was a low moaning, interspersed with a rapid singsong chant. Then he saw the machine-gun emplacement. It was off to their right, and the sounds emanated from its hidden interior.

As they slipped past it, Adam whispered, "The soldiers pray to their gods for protection against the mighty hand of the snake devil." So far so good, thought Jason. But the first burst of gunfire would alert the soldiers to their earthly jobs, and then things would get a bit tricky.

Leading the way, he crossed the remaining twenty yards to the edge of the net. It was staked down with metal pegs, an easier job than cutting through wire. A yank or two and they were inside. The laboratory was directly ahead, its windows blacked out from the inside. The prison compound was behind the building.

The door was unlocked and swung open. The place looked like a hospital. Followed by Cyber, Jason went down the antiseptically clean corridor, his footsteps echoing on the tiles. The hallway led past darkened examination rooms and a couple of small labs equipped with the usual paraphernalia for the treatment of human illness. At the far end was a turn. They reached it, and Jason stuck his head out and peered around.

The Chinese are bad disciplinarians all the way around, he thought. First they don't convince their troops that Communism is a better form of religion

132

than devil worship; second, they allow their guards to fall asleep on guard duty. He was looking at a snoring soldier, feet propped on a desk in front of a double set of green doors. The soldier had a machine gun, and its barrel was tickling his plump belly. Jason went forward on tiptoe until he was standing over the sleeping Chinese.

As everybody says all the time—sorry about this, he thought. His arm described a short, savage arc and the side of his rigid hand caught the Oriental across the back of his neck. He eased the unconscious soldier down to the floor, relieved him of his weapon, and motioned to Cyber. As he started toward the door he heard the first burst of gunfire. It was faint and coming from the direction of the airfield. Da Tenzing and his men were going into action.

The element of surprise was still riding with them, and Jason took full advantage of it. With Cyber behind him, he kicked open the double doors and stood looking down at the startled upturned faces of the men at work below.

He was standing on a steel platform overlooking a large, concrete-walled room. The floor was covered with machinery . . . mostly electronics, with wires and cables snaking everywhere. White-coated technicians were hunched over test benches, and the steady hum of high voltage filled the air. Then Jason saw something that made his blood run cold. One side of the room was given up to a row of small, double-barred, wire-enclosed cages. The occupants of the cages moved restlessly to and fro, like the monkeys that he had seen in zoos all over the world. From time to time they uttered anguished whimpering sounds, the expressions of age-old fear and pain. They were quite naked, and their bodies were covered with angry red welts, the marks of whips.

They were—or had once been—human beings.

Next to the cages a large inclined table with heavy straps was set up. It was surrounded by test-stands full of equipment that Jason recognized. A tall, white-coated figure moved through it, his back turned. He was even more familiar. It was Dr. Hsin Lau, and he was preparing to conduct another experiment with Jason Starr's stolen mind-control machine.

In the few seconds that had passed since his sudden appearance, only two or three of the Chinese had been alerted. Lau was still issuing instructions and the rest of the twenty or thirty people were busy with their mindless work. Then a warning yell echoed through the room. It came from Jason's left. He swing around and saw the man who had given it—a young Chinese who was in the process of drawing a Luger out of his belt.

There was no time to be polite.

Jason blew his chest to smoking ribbons with a short burst from the Thompson. The Chinese screamed once and slid under a lab table. Then the room erupted into a maelstrom of running, twisting, diving figures.

On the wall next to the cages there was a rack of weapons, undoubtedly for the protection of the hard-working torturers. Jason dropped down onto the platform and let them try to get to it. It wasn't quite fair, but it was the only way to convince them that he meant business. The Thompson stitched a pattern of death across the space in front of the gun-rack. The Chinese were quite fanatical about the whole thing; they kept on coming—and Jason kept on firing. They tried to divert him by throwing wrenches and other tools at his head, but he was well-protected by the height and the steel floor. Then they tried to electrocute him with a long, black cable that five of them carried, creeping forward across the shell-littered floor. He let them get within ten feet before he depressed the muzzle of the Thompson and ended their little party.

Then it was all over. Jason was surprised to see how few of the Chinese had decided that discretion was the better part of valor. Only three men stumbled forward out of the smoking shambles with their hands raised high over their heads. One of them was Dr. Hsin Lau.

The cold-eyed doctor stepped forward and let his hands fall to his sides. His face was an impassive mask. He looked neither startled nor particularly concerned. He looked like a man who has been annoyed by a temporary interruption. When he was standing in the middle of the floor he spoke. His English was pure, precise and cultivated, the hallmark of his British education.

"Ah, Mr. Jason Starr, if my surmise is correct . . . ? Your sudden appearance was rather startling . . . but, I must say, not totally unexpected. When your movements were traced to Simla by my good friend, Dr. Krupt, whom I believe you have met on one previous occasion, I suspected you might have gained information that would lead you here to my—ah—experimental hospital. Accordingly, I made arrangements for additional troops and protective measures. You have been a lucky man, so far." The doctor paused. His eyes narrowed into reptilian slits. "Mr. Starr," he continued, "it would be foolish for you to continue your one-man interference in the affairs of the Chinese government. Not only foolish—but unpleasantly fatal." Lau's voice sank into a malignant whisper.

"Lay down your weapon, Mr. Starr . . . there is a small chance that I may decide to save your life. I admire your courage—perhaps I shall be able to use it in more interesting ways."

Lau was playing for time, and Jason knew it. But what the Chinese didn't know was that his armed guards were being kept busy with Da Tenzing and his band of Sherpas. Still, the Sherpas couldn't hold off the Chinese forever, and Jason had to move quickly.

"Forget the compliments, Doctor, just put your arms up as high as they can reach or I'll arrange a nice little amputation ceremony for them." Jason gestured with the Thompson. The doctor obeyed with a tight-lipped smile. Covering him and the two dazed assistants, Jason moved down the steel steps to the main floor.

"Yes, this is quite a hospital you have here, doctor," Jason said, looking at the cages with their contents of human misery. "It rivals the best that the Gestapo ever created. But, then, you have Dr. Krupt to give you special advice in matters of torture."

"Torture, Mr. Starr?" Lau's smile changed into a frown. "The individuals you see are quartered inside security cells for their own protection. They are decrepit products of inbreeding among the ignorant tribes in the Tibetan Himalayas. Suitable subjects for my experiments—otherwise—" the doctor's voice rose shrilly—"unsuitable for anything but simple labor on the People's Communes."

"But suitable for experiments." Jason's voice held a deadly calm.

"Exactly. Thanks to your initial research." The doctor's head nodded at a table and, out of the corner of his eye, Jason saw the burnt remnants of the original equipment that had crashed with him in the jungles of South Viet Nam. "Yes, because of your brilliant discoveries, Mr. Starr, we have been able to improve and increase the strength of the thought-generator to one thousand times its original capacity. When broadcast over thousands of miles it will cast a net of confusion over entire continents. All that remains for us to do is to reduce the size of the equipment so that it can be encapsuled inside of a small orbiting satellite."

The man was mad. He was also full of deadly intelligence . . . the kind of intelligence that considered mass murder or mass mind-destruction a simple means to an end.

"Yes, that's a very bright idea," said Jason. "Too bad the world isn't quite ready for it. Now, Doctor, if you don't mind—just turn around—nice and slowly—that's it—press your hands up against that wall—and don't move a muscle or I'll feel an urgent need to shoot your backside off." Jason snapped out the words. The doctor's face changed into a mask of hatred. For a second, Jason thought the madman was going to spring at him. His finger tightened on the trigger. Then, with a shrug of his thin shoulders, Lau followed the instructions.

"You are a fool. You will die slowly and terribly." His cultured voice filtered through the hum of the machinery.

The doctor had a point, thought Jason. Time was running out. But it no longer mattered whether he lived or died . . . died for the second time, this time permanently. The important thing was to destroy the mind-control equipment. What to do with Lau could wait for later.

Motioning to Cyber, who was still standing on the platform, Jason told him to bring the rucksack with the demolition charges. Working swiftly, Jason placed them, attached the radio detonators, and returned to take over the job of guarding Lau and his fellow workers.

"Take my black boxes up into the outside hall; they might come in handy as proof . . . if we get out of here alive," Jason told his companion. Cyber collected them from their table and started toward the exit. Before he had taken three steps, the sound of machine guns firing outside the building vibrated through the walls of the laboratory. The gun crews had finally seen through the practical joke. The explosions set off a chain reaction of gibbering growls from the inside of the cages.

"You see, Mr. Starr, your resistance is pointless." The doctor's cool, taunting voice rose over the intermittent firing.

Jason ignored him. Time had run out at last. They would never leave the building alive. But, then, neither would Lau. It was probably better that way. As much as he was disgusted by the contents of the cages, slaughtering humans—completely deformed physically and mentally as they were—was not a pleasant idea. It would be a quick and merciful act to do the job, and if he had to he would share the death at the same time. Jason's finger caressed the button on the small detonating transmitter. He looked at his friend, the man from the future. Cyber understood. He smiled his acknowledgment and his head nodded.

Then two things happened so quickly that Jason could only stand numbly and watch.

The door to the laboratory burst open, and a man who looked as if he had been put through a meat-cutter plunged into the room. His face streaming with hundreds of tiny cuts, his clothes in tatters, and holding a Sten gun at the ready, Otto Krupt stood, glaring at the shambles below.

At the same instant Dr. Lau moved.

With snakelike speed the Chinese launched himself across the five feet that separated him from the barred doors of the cage. Before Jason could react, the doctor had flipped the crossbar up and pulled back the heavy mesh screen. Then it was too late to do anything at all. Krupt was covering them, and the howling horde of half-men were springing out of the open prison to the floor.

"The detonating device, and your weapon, Mr. Starr," Krupt's hoarse voice was full of triumph. "I will blow you to shreds before your finger moves enough to set off the charge. Put them down. Gently, please."

Jason put the box on the floor. He looked at Cyber. His friend's eyes were closed and his head was swaying slightly. It was hopeless. A feeling of despair welled in Jason's throat. He should have destroyed the laboratory without bothering to battle his conscience. Now it was too late.

"Move toward me, Mr. Starr," Krupt ordered. "And your sly friend. Hein!" he snapped.

As he started to walk toward the platform, Jason could hear Dr. Lau behind him, opening the rack of hunting rifles. Then he heard a sound that made his head snap around quickly. It was a low growl followed by the scream of an enraged animal on the attack.

Lau was crouching in front of the wall, his hands working feverishly over the jammed mechanism of a high-powered rifle. Five naked, hairy men were moving in on him, their throats rumbling with savage sounds as old as the jungle. A small hope started to build in Jason's mind. He swung around again and looked up at the German.

Krupt was showing signs of confusion. It had been

139

a long day for the leader of the Brotherhood. His hand came up and wiped the blood streaming from the cuts on his forehead out of his eyes. The Sten wavered, trying to cover both Jason and Adam as well as the brain-washed Tibetans who were now closing in on the frantic Chinese.

Events made his decision for him. It was the wrong decision.

As Dr. Lau's first terrified scream welled up from behind Jason, the German raised his gun and fired a long burst into the group of snarling creatures who were in the process of repaying their master's cruelty. It was the chance that Jason had been waiting for.

As the German fired his second burst into the struggling, snapping mass of half-men, he launched himself in a low dive toward the still-sputtering high-voltage electric cable . . . the cable that had been carried to within ten feet of his former perch on the steel platform by a group of now-dead Chinese.

It had to be well-timed, and it was. Jason's dive carried him to within three feet of the exposed end. As his shoulder hit the floor, one hand closed on the thick wire four inches below the live tip. Then he was rolling over and coming up, legs churning toward the closest support of the platform.

A half-second before the tip slapped against the steel girder, the firing stopped. Krupt must have seen it, Jason thought, as his body hurtled by under the overhead and his arm slapped the wire against the steel. Then he slammed into the concrete wall, shoulder first, and lay dazed for a long moment, hearing the crackle and smelling the acrid odor of the ozone generated by 20,000 volts coursing through the metal platform.

He lay there until his head stopped trying to explode. Then he crawled back out and stood up. His eyes flicked over to the opposite side of the room. It wasn't a very pleasant sight. The half-men had taken what was left of Dr. Lau back inside their cage. They were now busily distributing portions of it to the other members of the group. Cyber was still standing where he had been moments before. His eyes were open again, and his face looked white. It was the first time Jason had seen the man from the future react so obviously to violence.

"We'd better try to get out of here," he said. Then he ripped the sputtering cable from its contact with the steel platform. He looked up.

The platform was empty.

Somehow, Krupt had managed to jump back through the door in time. Swiftly Jason retrieved his weapon and the detonator. With Cyber behind him, he raced up the steps. If Krupt was waiting in the hall, the German would have his Sten gun zeroed in on the doorway. Jason took a chance. He stuck his head around the corner and took a quick look.

The hallway was empty. Both Krupt and the guard had fled. The firing outside the building had stopped. It was mysteriously quiet. As he and Cyber rounded the second corner in the hospital's hall, they were met by a familiar sound. It was the happy laughter of Da Tenzing, booming through the vacant building.

The Sherpa chief was at the head of the hall with three of his companions. His face was covered with powder burns and he looked a bit wobbly. But his good humor was still keeping his bruised exterior from seeking rest.

"Ah, my friend, we are temporarily the winners," he boomed. "The Chinese dogs have been driven into the network of trenches. My men can hold them for perhaps a half-hour. Have you found that which you search for?"

Jason explained quickly. When he finished, the Sherpa nodded his understanding.

"Then we shall begin to organize a path of retreat," he said. "The sons of devils have maintained control of their radio, and it will not be easy to recross the border."

"Wait!" Jason cut in. "The airstrip—is it still in our hands?" An idea was beginning to take shape in his mind. A crazy idea, but with the Chinese alerting their border forces and reserve elements, one that he felt worth the risk.

"Yes, at least for the moment. And the aircraft is undamaged. If we but had the skills to operate it, our escape would be simple."

The old DC-3. A simple machine . . . that is if you knew anything about flying two-engined aircraft. Jason didn't. His only experience had been a few hours of flying lessons at the controls of a Piper Cub in his days at the RAND Corporation. He had never even found the time to get his license. Yet, if he could get her into the air, he could probably fly her. The DC-3 was the most forgiving aircraft ever built. Landing again was something there was no time to worry about.

"Da Tenzing, get your men ready for a quick exit." He decided it. "I've just elected myself a member of the airline pilots' association."

Telling the Sherpa to get his men to the airstrip, Jason and Adam stayed inside the empty hospital for a few more minutes. Now that he had the proof he needed to convince the CIA, there was something else . . . something almost as important, and Jason decided that the delay was worth the risk.

Cyber found the safe. It was in plain sight, inside the most luxurious office. Probably Dr. Lau's, thought Jason, watching his friend's fingers swirl through the intricate combination as if it were a child's penny puzzle. The door swung open and Jason went to work on the contents of heavy, sealed folders. He discarded right and left. It was mostly records of day-to-day experiments, interesting and valuable but not what he was looking for. When he found what he was looking for, a cloth-covered file marked *Property of the People's Secret Service*, there was no time to examine its contents. The firing was beginning again, and it was time to leave.

When they emerged from the building, Jason was surprised to see that it was growing light. The night had been short and full of violence. When they were clear of the camouflage and running toward the dim outlines of the airstrip and the parked plane, Jason did what he had regretted doing just a half-hour previously.

He pressed the detonator. A flash and a roar followed. Then a series of hollow explosions. The acrid smell of burning fuel oil reached Jason's nose. Diesel-fuel storage tanks for the electrical generating plant, he thought.

His thoughts turned toward the red-haired German. Otto Krupt was somewhere near and, now, there was no time to settle old accounts. Perhaps in the future, thought Jason.

He ran on, clutching the heavy file and stumbling over the rocky ground. He didn't bother to look back.

As THE REMAINING Chinese launched an all-out assault against the last machine-gun emplacement that stood between them and the escaping aircraft, Jason heard the number-two engine sputter and stall for the third time. He frantically punched the priming button, moved the mixture to full-rich and tried again. The old crate had been sitting all night and the oil was half-frozen. Beside him, Cyber looked out into the dawn-bright sky. There wasn't much for him to do—getting the DC-3 airborne was essentially a one-man operation, so far not much more complicated than a modern single-engined procedure.

As Da Tenzing's two volunteers in the machine-gun emplacement sprayed a stream of tracers toward the attacking Chinese, the engine finally caught and blew a cloud of flame out of its rusty manifold. There was no time for a warm-up. Hoping she wouldn't stall again, Jason released the emergency brake and gave number one the gun, and the old bird lurched around and moved down the taxiway toward the runway. Behind his shoulder the Sherpa leader grunted in satisfaction. His men were strapped in along the sides of the cabin.

By the time Jason had turned onto the short strip and was heading down to turn around for the takeoff, the two brave men who had elected to stay behind were dead and the distant figures running toward the field were the first of the Chinese. Trying to remember what came next, Jason glanced at the manifold pressure gauges. They seemed to be somewhere near the proper readings. Temperature looked okay. Flaps at fifteen degrees. Prop-pitch full, mixture—too rich —his hand fiddled with the knobs until the engine smoothed out. There was supposed to be a tail-wheel lock somewhere. He had once heard an RAF pilot complaining about its tendency to stay locked. The hell with it, he decided. It was time to get moving. His hand moved across the dual throttles and shoved them all the way forward. He let his toes relax across the brakes, and the old airplane shuddered slowly forward, its engines drumming through the thin walls of the cockpit.

Steer with your brakes until you can control her with the tail surfaces . . . wheel in neutral . . . she'll fishtail a little . . . don't worry about it . . . now you're picking up speed . . . wheel forward to bring her nose level . . . hold it there . . . don't let her get off the ground until she can fly . . . keep your eyes down the middle of the runway . . . let the view take care of itself. Jason heard the voice of his old instructor, coaching, encouraging, explaining. . . . now you're close . . . now ease back . . . just a little . . . that's all it takes . . . she'll lift herself like a bird . . . you're doing fine . . . relax . . . relax . . .

They were five feet, ten feet . . . fifty feet off the runway, the ground whizzing past his window. They were in the sky, and Jason let his breathing return to a half-normal state. Slowly and carefully he retracted the landing gear, the flaps, and then he powered back and thinned out the fuel mixture. They were climbing up toward the knife-edged ridges of Nanda Devi, now outlined in the morning sunlight, with the lake down below on their left and a rising column of black oil smoke marking the secret laboratory.

Jason swung the nose away from the menacing peaks of the sacred mountain and headed northwest, following the wide gorge that had been carved out by the headwaters of the Indus river. The old DC-3 was unpressurized and had no superchargers; it would never make it over the tops of the 25,000-foot peaks that enclosed the valley.

Their present course was free of obstacles for a few miles, and he had some map reading to do.

"Adam," he said, "just hold her where she is . . . it's like driving a car." By the time he remembered that Adam had never driven a car, it was too late—his friend was flying the airplane, smoothly and naturally . . . as if it was another primitive toy with which he could amuse himself for a few moments.

Jason had a look at the Chinese pilot's map case. The course they were following would take them out of the mountains into the disputed territory of Kashmir. Another hundred miles would put them inside the Pakistani border. Since there was no choice —in the other direction lay the really high mountains and China—he decided.

"Da Tenzing," he said to the Sherpa who was peering curiously over his shoulder, "if we land in Indian-held Kashmir, the plane and everything in it will be confiscated. The Indians don't want any trouble with their Chinese neighbors . . . at least not this kind of trouble. On the other hand, the Pakistanis have had it up to here as far as their Chinese friends are concerned. If we're lucky we can make Peshawar and leave the explanations to the U.S. government."

"That is true," the Sherpa said, without his characteristic smile. "However, we are Indians, we will be detained—perhaps imprisoned by the Pakistanis. Such is the way of governments in opposition to each other."

The Sherpa was right, thought Jason. Because of the border dispute, he and his men stood a good chance of being arrested as spies or for whatever else the Moslems decided was a convenient excuse.

"I'm sorry I got you into this, Da Tenzing. Looks like we'll have to find another country to land in," he said.

"Wait!" The Sherpa's face suddenly lit up. He disappeared through the door to the main cabin. Seconds later, he was back, now grinning broadly.

"You will land where you please . . . and we will land in Kashmir," he said.

"What do you mean?"

"Parachutes. Enough for all of us. I have made many jumps during the war and I, Da Tenzing, will instruct my men in the proper methods."

Jason's eyes moistened slightly, but he didn't disagree. He took back the controls from Cyber as the plane bored into the narrowing eye of the first high-walled gorge.

Flying through the Indus River canyon was like threading a needle with a runaway locomotive. The walls grew closer and meaner; downdrafts sucked the old bird perilously close to the foaming rapids that plunged through the sheer, living rock; updrafts pushed Jason halfway through his seat, and he could see the wing tips bending and contorting in ways that Douglas had never intended. Well, it's one way to get the hang of rock formation flying in a two-engine airplane, thought Jason, his hands constantly busy with trim tabs, power settings and pitch controls. A very dangerous way, too.

It wasn't much fun for the passengers. Da Tenzing's face changed color, and he tried to keep his grin going. The effort failed, and the white-faced Sherpa disappeared into the cabin to share his air-sickness with his men. Cyber was immune to it all. He had produced a paperback copy of Borel's *Space and Time*, and as the walls of the gorge whizzed by only a few feet from his face, he was reading it at his usual clip.

After an hour of it, the walls receded and the gorge widened out into a valley. They were approaching the Indian-Kashmiri border. Jason relaxed. It looked like a milk run from now on. Da Tenzing had his men into their chutes. Jason started to gain altitude for the jump. Then he saw the contrail out of his starboard window. It was high and moving three times as fast as the old C-47. It grew larger until he caught the flash of sun on silver wings. It was coming out of Tibet. The Chinese were making a last-ditch attempt to retrieve their honor and to destroy the evidence.

It was the time for quick decisions. The jet looked like a late-model MIG, a supersonic job, good for high-altitude pursuit work. Maybe not so good for low and slow infighting. Jason was at 1,500 feet. He shoved the control column forward and dove the shuddering old bird toward the flat surface of the valley.

The MIG was close now, and he could see the red star on its delta wing. It was above and ahead of him, sweeping into a high-speed turn. The pilot would try to get behind him if he knew his business. Jason was skimming a hundred feet above the flat valley floor. He watched the jet complete its turn and disappear from his line of sight. Motioning Da Tenzing to climb up into the navigation bubble behind the pilot's seat, he waited. The Sherpa would have to be his eyes from now on.

"The jackal approaches," Da Tenzing called out. "He is a mile behind . . . now a half-mile . . ."

Jason twisted the wheel savagely and gave the engines full power. Now that he was getting the feel of her, his confidence was growing. The plane whipped over on its wingtip in a steep bank just above the rushing earth. Two seconds later, a stream of tracers exploded off to the left in the empty sky where the old C-47 should have been. Then the MIG flashed by them and Jason caught a glimpse of a fiercely concentrating face. Error number one, he thought. Never lose your temper during the ball game.

He leveled off. On his new course, he was heading toward the mountains that ringed the valley. They were two or three miles away, just about perfect for his next tactic. Keeping the plane low, he traced the maneuvers of his angry Chinese friend.

The Chinese pilot was indeed upset. He had been scrambled out of a warm bed to chase an obsolete plane with orders to destroy it. Orders that made no allowance for failure. He was a relatively good pilot. He had been trained to operate high in the stratosphere. But now the ground was close and the speed of his aircraft made him nervous. He circled again and dove towards the slow-moving propeller-driven airplane. Because he had been trained and over-trained in the techniques of high-altitude, maximum-power approaches, his hand automatically moved the throttle forward. The MIG leaped ahead as the afterburner cut in. His finger started to depress the trigger for his twenty-millimeter cannons.

The mountains were very close, now, and Jason

held the nose toward the nearest ridge. Da Tenzing was calling out the range of the approaching jet in an excited series of shouts.

"Two miles . . . one mile . . . the dog has activated his afterburners!" The Sherpa yelled.

A couple of seconds later, Jason yanked the control column all of the way in to his stomach and the C-47 lurched into a steep climb, its engine protesting but doing the job. The ridge was a sheer wall just ahead and Jason skinned across its top with a few feet to spare. In the long moment that followed, he noticed his hands. They were trembling.

"Ai-yah!" shouted Da Tenzing. "The fool has gone right into the mountain!"

Jason swung the plane around and headed back into the valley. As he recrossed the top of the ridge he looked down. A great ball of flames marked the grave of the MIG. It had hit well below the top of the ridge. The explosion had started a small landslide, and he could see charred pieces of wreckage tumbling slowly to the valley floor.

He relaxed. It hadn't been such a milk run after all.

"In five minutes you'll jump," he told the Sherpa.

The goodbyes were brief but deeply felt. Without Da Tenzing, his mission would have ended in failure. The Sherpas were a brave people. Seven of them had given their lives without a question. Now it was time to deposit them in safe territory.

He watched the chutes blossom over the fertile plain and slowly become distant specks, lost in the haze. Peshawar lay a hundred miles ahead. And after Peshawar, there was some unfinished business to take care of. Business in Washington, D.C., with a man who Jason knew quite well . . . a man who had spent twenty years of his life serving his government because it was a family tradition. A man who had used people as if they were bugs, to be squashed when their functions ceased to be necessary.

Jason thought of Joe Blake, of Kumindani, and of Mr. Chatterji's last plea for a merciful death. He thought of the Brotherhood and Otto Krupt. Krupt was free, but not for long. He would have to answer to his superiors, who never gave their agents a second chance. Or, perhaps, someday he would answer to Jason. But the man who had so neatly arranged for his murder and who sat, now, behind his well-polished desk inside the CIA was the most dangerous man of all.

The man's name was Hamilton, and the secret file nestled against Jason's leg told the whole story. As the plane droned on, Jason's mind was far away. He was a man in a hurry and a girl named Maria d'Allesandro Corday was in great danger . . . if not already dead.

Now, he thought, all I have to do is get this bird into Pakistani territory and, hopefully, on the ground in one piece.

Chapter †
SIXTEEN

LIKE INDIA, Washington was used to the heat. The city sweltered under the July sun and the Capitol dome shimmered through the mid-morning glare. The President was on his ranch, and half the city was on vacation. Little boys dove into the stone pools below the fountains, searching for coolness and pennies while endless streams of tourists took pictures.

Jason called the CIA from the airport. He asked for Maria.

"I'm sorry, sir, Miss Corday isn't in this week," the receptionist told him. "She's on vacation."

"And Mr. Hamilton?"

"Mr. Hamilton has been ill for the last two days—"

Jason hung up. He called Maria's apartment. There was no answer. Two days. The two days that had passed since he had put the old C-47 down in Pakistan, a rough landing but good enough to leave the plane in one piece. The two days that it had taken Jason to untangle his affairs with the American embassy and hop the commercial flight to the United States. Time enough for Hamilton to be informed.

Turning to Adam Cyber, he gave him the briefcase containing the secret dossier he had taken from the Chinese laboratory and the shattered remnants of his thought-control device.

"How you do it is your problem, Adam, but get these to the Deputy Director of the Central Intelligence Agency as fast as you can. It's the proof they've been screaming for. Plus the fact that one of their most trusted officials has been a double agent for the past twenty years. I'm heading for the Hamilton estate."

The Hamilton estate was surrounded by miles of woodland. The road grew narrower with each twist, and tree branches scraped across the top of Jason's car. When he saw the gate, he stopped and backed up until the car was out of sight behind a curve. He struck off through the woods, trying to keep his feet from cracking dried branches and hoping that time hadn't run out.

If Hamilton had had two days, the old man was probably long gone. Neither Jason nor the CIA would ever hear of him again. And Maria—the girl was the hostage that Hamilton had chosen just in case his game backfired.

The house was an Elizabethan monstrosity. Four floors of leaded windows, ornate chimney pots, and flaking plaster. The driveway was empty, and the house looked as if no one had lived in it for fifty years. Jason remembered that Hamilton had been known as Washington's most unpopular socialite. Now he could see why. It was the perfect cover. He let himself in through a window that opened into a baronial dining hall with a table thirty feet long and a fireplace big enough for a man to stand up in. The place was empty, dusty and unused. It reminded Jason of the Mogul palace in New Delhi. He crept forward toward the half-open door that gave way into the entrance hall.

His head poked around the door-frame. That was as far as it got. Something kicked him across the back of the neck with paralyzing force. It was an odd feeling. His eyes were open but his body was numb. He was falling toward the floor, noticing, idly, that it needed a good coat of wax. Then things grew black.

The perfume was familiar. He smelled it before he could get his eyes open. Finally he managed the left one. When the room stopped spinning, he tried the right. They both worked fine, and only the ache across the back of his neck reminded him that something had nearly killed him in one blow. Yes, his eyes were working perfectly and they were looking into another pair . . . a pair of aquamarine eyes in a beautiful and sensual face. It was Maria d'Allesandro Corday, and the .45-caliber automatic in her delicate hand was pinpointing the spot midway between his temples.

"I'm terribly sorry, Jason," she said. Her eyes told him that she was. At least in a small way.

"That's nice," he said. "I'm glad we can still be friends."

"Oh, yes, Mr. Starr, let us not allow ourselves to become embittered. It is the fortunes of war," the deep voice of Winslow J. Hamilton said from across the room. Jason looked. The CIA chief was putting the finishing touches on a large black oil drum. Two wires led out of the lid, and Hamilton was connecting them to what Jason recognized as a simple time-detonating mechanism.

"A jury-rigged device, Mr. Starr. But then you gave us such short notice," said Hamilton. He finished his connections and stood up. Jason looked at Maria.

"Why?" he said.

"For money, Jason. For the world that I want, the world where money buys any future you can dream of. But you wouldn't understand," Maria's eyes were steady and cold.

154

"I suppose not," he said. "Too bad money can't buy you a clean conscience and too bad about the thousands of people that your friend over there has eliminated over the years."

"Don't waste the girl's time, Mr. Starr," said Hamilton. "She knows what she wants." His hand caught Maria's long black hair and stroked it. Maria smiled.

"Mr. Starr, you have done quite well for an amateur," Hamilton continued. "Where others have failed, you have destroyed my cover. A cover that began twenty years ago when I was substituted for the real Mr. Hamilton, unfortunately long deceased. You have also succeeded in destroying Doctor Hsin Lau and his experimental records. For this and for many other reasons, you will have to die, Mr. Starr. Although we realize the game is up, your death will leave certain problems unresolved. For instance, the thought-control device . . . The world will have to wait until the Chinese people succeed in remaking it. This may take a long time . . . but we are a patient nation."

"Yes," said Jason. "A bunch of torturers and murderers working on a long-term contract to dominate the human race."

"Enough!" snapped Hamilton. "Maria, tie him. Tie him securely. Mr. Starr, there is enough high explosive in the barrel to eliminate you and my house. By the time the explosion is investigated, Maria and I will be landing in my helicopter fifty miles off the Eastern shore of Maryland. A submarine is waiting there to take us home."

The girl worked swiftly. She knew her business. When she had finished, Jason was trussed up into a ball of protesting muscle.

"You have approximately a half-hour, Mr. Starr. To be humane, I should shoot you now, but this will

155

repay Doctor Lau's horrible death in a small way," said Hamilton.

"One question," said Jason. "Why was Maria almost murdered in my hotel room?" He was hoping the question would have some effect on the girl. It did.

She laughed.

"Even professionals make mistakes," she said. "The fools who planted the gas capsule were instructed to leave the safety on. It was my task to activate it just before I left you to enjoy your well-earned rest." She laughed again. Ironically, the woman whom Jason had almost loved was as deadly as the snake that had killed Mr. Chatterji.

"Come, Maria," ordered Hamilton. "Let Mr. Starr enjoy his last moments alone."

Jason watched them leave. A minute later he heard the helicopter engine start out in back of the house. Then it lifted and the noise faded away. Except for the ticking of the detonator, the room was silent. He struggled against the rope, thinking of Maria and Hamilton, now on their way to safety. He cursed himself aimlessly. It was too late. But at least now his name would be cleared and the CIA would take steps to keep a closer eye on the Chinese developments in brain research. He continued to fight the ropes, but it was no use. Maria had done a perfect job.

"No, my friend, not quite perfect." A voice broke the stillness. Footsteps sounded behind Jason. "My —ah—business with the Deputy Director of the CIA took less time than I expected," said Adam Cyber.

"Adam, before you say another word, disconnect that detonator," said Jason.

"And how the hell did you get here?" he asked as Cyber finished his work over in the corner.

"It was necessary to learn how to operate one of your ground vehicles," said the man from the future. "I fear that my proficiency is not good and that the policeman who followed me will shortly arrive." Adam smiled as if the idea was quite amusing.

The traffic cop did arrive. He pulled up on his motorcycle and cut the siren just as Jason and Adam were coming out of the front door of Hamilton's mansion.

"Never mind the explanations, buddy," he began.

"Officer, do you have a radio on that bike?" Jason broke in.

"What do you think this is—the sixteenth century? Of course," the officer said.

"Then get me through to your headquarters. This is a matter of national security. You can write your ticket afterwards," said Jason.

"Say, just what the hell is going on?" The officer was looking upset.

"A promotion for you, if you do as I ask," said Jason.

That seemed to make the policeman feel better. He called his headquarters, and a few minutes later Jason was talking to the Deputy Director of the CIA. When he had explained the situation there was silence at the other end for a moment. Then the Director came back.

"It checks out, all right," he said. "The Air Defense Command has a slow-moving blip on their scopes. It's headed out to sea . . . already about twenty-five miles offshore. We've scrambled an interceptor. He's over them now. Wait a minute, I think we can listen in."

The static-filtered voice of a hunter-killer pilot came through the police radio.

"Angel-two to Big Brother . . . it's a whirlybird,

no markings, headed out to sea . . . trying to raise them on the radio . . ."

Jason listened.

". . . this is an Air Force intercept," he heard the pilot say. ". . . you are ordered to return at once to the nearest safe landing area . . ."

There was more silence. Then the pilot reported.

". . . Angel-two to Big Brother . . . there's no answer, but they got the message . . . they've gone as low as they can go."

The Deputy Director's voice cut in.

"All right," he said. "Follow your instructions."

". . . Roger . . . am launching one Genie air-to-air rocket with high-explosive warhead." The pilot sang out.

It seemed like a long time before his voice came in again.

"Jesus! . . . . it was a direct hit . . . no sign of the copter . . . I'm circling the area now . . . am waiting for further instructions . . ."

"Angel-two, this is Big Brother. Return to base," a new voice cut in.

"Roger, returning to base. Out." The pilot's voice faded away.

It was all over. Hamilton and the girl had become part of the restless ocean. A swift and terrible death. Jason didn't want to think about it. He was suddenly very tired. He wanted to sleep. Then he wanted to have a drink and talk to a woman who would smile without death in her eyes.

"Sign your ticket and come on," he said to Adam. "We'll stay at the Ambassador, this time."

A few hours later, Jason and Adam were sitting inside a bar overlooking the swimming pool. Adam was sampling his first Scotch and soda and Jason was thinking about the CIA's offer to reinstate him with the RAND Corporation. "It's the very least we can do to rectify our error, Mr. Starr," the Deputy Director had told him. "And I think you should consider it carefully. The government needs men like you . . . even though it sometimes fails to listen to them." It was a fair admission, thought Jason, looking down at a long-stemmed girl in a bikini that didn't leave much of her trim body to the imagination. But he had all but made his decision. The RAND Corporation was a splendid place to spend a lifetime of desk sitting and theorizing. But too much had happened too swiftly for him to go back to it.

"Well, Adam, now that your work is finished, I guess you will be—returning," said Jason. Yes, he thought. Returning fifty thousand years to seek out other trouble spots in history and try to rectify the mistakes before they changed the pattern.

His Mind Brother's face was absorbed in the investigation of the strange-tasting liquor. He looked up and Jason saw the corners of his lips break into an ironic smile.

"I'm afraid, my friend, that is impossible," he said. "There is no one to operate the dilation apparatus . . . It was a one-way trip, as you say here in the twentieth century. Besides, I would like to work with you."

"Then you can't go back. You're here forever . . ." said Jason.

His Mind Brother smiled. "Yes," he said. "But forever is *not* such a long, long time."